ARTAI
Books and Litery Arts

ABIKÚ

The Novel

DELE BLISS PAAGO

Author of *Afrikaman*

Published in Nigeria, 2021

ARTAFRIKA
Port-Harcourt. Lagos. Nairobi.

Acknowledgement

I owe special debt to my grandfather's library where first I found Homer and Virgil and a perpetual dissatisfaction with African literature. I thank Mallam Hassan for his copy of Garcia's "One Hundred Years of Solitude".

I frequently talked over the concepts in this book with my father, Elder V.I Paago and with Elizabeth Chindah -their encouragement or confusion helped steer me aright so any flaws are of my obstinacy. I thank my Mother, my five siblings and the Imabel family for loving support.

Friends helped me. There are the estranged ones bound within the characters; others kind enough to run errands; and those like Becky Chi Ehoro, Akin Wunmi, Showunmi Rofiat, Olojo Olawale, Gbemiga Idahosa, Abiodun Oyedepo, Toluse Zion, Jeffery Ikhide and Ibukun Atolagbe who offered direct assistance in research and accomodation or offered ideas.

Mr. Bamidele Ojo sparked my teenage interest in history, Hon. Bayo Ishola in politics, Seun Adepoju in philosophy, Adama Joshua in activism, Sam Dedetoku in panAfricanism and Patrick Naagbanton in journalism.

Beyond reach, I announce my debt to Abani Chris, Charles Hill, Wole Soyinka, T.E Lawrence, J.P Clark and Ben Okri.

My brief stint in poetry and theatre, the ventures into entrepreneurship, tedious career in teaching and consultancy, and this abiding interest in politics has unconsciously followed the path of a childhood hero: Ken Saro-Wiwa.

Dr. Odeh of the Department of History introduced me to the Unilorin Staff Club and I gained, in one evening, greater understanding of Lagos than is evident in most books. I thank him and the two Aboyeji brothers and their rare solicitude for the ambitious young.

For any depth of feeling in Book II, I owe special thanks to Biafranwarmemories.com. Government-sanctioned books are one thing and Chika Oduah's project a refreshing other. My understanding of yoruba native practices began under the Femi Obamero's tutelage.

Dele Bliss Paago

Then there is something divine; evident and speaking in the dreams of night, vague and abrupt in light. Muse, Daemon or Alter, I thank whatever binds you to me. I thank you.

To Father,

the Earthly, the Divine.

Disclaimer

The persons and events represented here do not follow facts in time, act or place. There is no measure of truth here beyond the sheer necessity of this novel's idea.

But how does that matter to us, dear reader? Close your eyes and hear my of the tortoise. It is no small secret, I tell you.

The Sun came up upon the left

Out of the Sea came he!

And he shone bright, and on the right

Went down into the sea.

SAMUEL TAYLOR COLERIDGE

The Rime of the Ancient Mariner

TABLE OF CONTENTS

FOUNTAIN

"**A**re you not tired of the sea?"

You hear alot of things at the university, imprisoned minds can scarce be sane, but I looked up from my bagel in the manner of an appreciative connoiseur with a new specimen.

"Am I not tired of the sea?" I asked self, tasted it, this new brand of madness -a lecturer from the marine department perhaps.

I abadoned the hypothesis. He looked like a bum in danshiki. One of those poor bastards in African Juju then. Or an outcast like myself.

I was sitting at Fountain 33. I could remember no reason for the name, it was neither fountain nor one of many. This was the university square for the modern jew, sunshine for the riverine swine, common-room of the suspect minorities of the Free States of Biafra.

He felt like faculty. Emperor Hitsu had his Unit 731 and the Germans had conducted racial science. The Free States of Biafra, had pressed a class of scholars into service to build a tradi-scientific belief system. Juju.

They were granted funds and the endless stream of bodies from saboteurs. The experiments were legendary. The Wirths even more so -*Afa* left them crippled, dumb, mad. He was none of these things.

"Are you not?"

"I guess I am" I answered with unease. These were not times to talk about the sea anyhow.

The government could invite you for questioning and you would not return. Or you did and remained a ghost, avoided by neighbours and friends -*wetin hin bin give them to come atside?*

"Who are you?"

"I come from the other side" Definitely one of those poor bastards in African Juju.

Or a trap, an informer. I looked around – *what other side? Nigeria and sabotage? The resistance?* But it was a fine afternoon - the closest third a student amply concerned with the bossom of his classmate.

I had a bagel, leisure and sunlight -rare pleasures for an outcast -and I wanted to humour him "What's on the other side?"

"The pot." Okay. I shrugged, figured I deserved that for engaging a crakpot. I needed to go anyway. My chest was burning again.

He saw my new dis-interest and explained "the pot is where the sea comes from, the vessel of the Goddess, the navel of fate"

"Nice"

"It is important. The time has come again"

I laughed "time has come for what?". Better to draw attention with a loud voice. One did not want a midnight knock from NDI Agents. I laughed loud. "What are you talking about?"

He brought out a bitter kola from his hunter's bag and began to shell it slowly. A crude way to ferment curiosity, I presumed. I turned away.

"24 Ube Street. Come there and I will show you the pot"

If this is how the resistance recruited people, they could be no more than a circus outfit. I wanted to tell him something distinctly impolite about chamber-pots and his head but I turned to him and he was gone. He was gone, I tell you.

"Are you not tired of the sea?"

To make a man run mad, give him an idea in endless loop. The sea was suddenly everywhere, in memory and in the classroom, a student complaining that "they were at sea" with my method, to shouts of "hear,hear".

It was in the Yoruba play to which the Department of Theatre Arts had invited me "Omo Olokun". Olokun's child. Olokun, Goddess of the Sea.

It was in the news, the Biafran Navy had lost a schooner at sea and blamed the Nigerian Government. The sea-port on the Niger was slated for dredging and environmentalists were protesting.

It was in my dreams, terrifying moments of drowning and I would wake up clawing my way out of a damp bed. Wicked, that is what it was. My sanity put to sea.

The day I found myself running to Fountain33 because an impromptu meeting had taken lunch, I knew I would go see him.

It had been two weeks but the address was seared across my soul and if the danshiki-bum turned out to be a spy and the sea something which involved disappearance, I would at-least have curiosity sated.

For precaution however, I told Doctor Abbe. He carefully noted our conversation in the presence of two graduate assistants -one could not be too careful in times like these – gave copies to his private and departmental secretaries, then informed me he would play bat-man.

He was departmental head for Political Science and pure-blood Ibo, a taciturn fellow like myself, the sort to attend a wine-party and sit at the corner in observation, the sort the National Department of Intelligence left alone.

After several years of evening school, my devotion had been rewarded with the minorities chair in political history. He was singlehandedly responsible. A good man.

But our friendship was a tame affair, did not warrant this danger. "You could disappear" I told him. I wanted him with me.

"Doesn't matter how a good story ends"

"You could disappear" I repeated with my most earnest look.

"Your poor attempts at acting are why you are in that department of the dead and unuseful. When are we going?"

"Tomorrow, after classes" I thought for a moment "Two Cars?" I asked him.

"Just mine" I thanked God. Gas was expensive these days.

We set out at dusk; 24 Ube Street was along a stretch called D-line, no great distance from the campus, and found a small squat house.

We knocked and a maid in white wrapper presently came to the door, profuse with apologies, her bare feet ringed with chalk indicating something more than a sanatorium nurse. She did not ask us any questions but continued in sonorous whisper of apologies as she led us into the parlor.

I found my voice when she asked us if we wanted tea. Yes.

Yes, Tea.

The house was quiet. The brick walls were eighteen inches thick, the doors of solid oak had turned silently on crafty hinges and our foot-falls were muted by elegant rugs.

The sitting room held no television. Chairs and a chandelier, magazines, a grand piano --when the maid gestured to a sofa, I picked The New York Times off the closest stool. 12 Jan 1970. It fell open to page 12: "Nigerian War at a Glance".

I breathed a sigh of relief. If this fellow was pro-Biafra, I was safe from charges of sabotage. It now remained to see what he wanted, perhaps decline without the charge of treason. *Lese-majesty* was a broad term these days.

A shrine is a peculiar place. Sanitation is detrimental, the doors are low and it forces you to whisper. There are spiritual reasons for physical objects and the rules.

If the babalawo does not look up when you enter, note it. The doors are low to force your respect. Things move and test your reaction. If the babalawo does not look down when you leave, note it.

I had been to one, many years ago. To get a job at the university, applicants had to swear oaths -secrecy and a percentage of one's salary to the benefactor.

The native doctor asked the spirits about us. His primary deity hung in the centre of the shrine as a ball on a vertical string. It was obstinate. He would ask it to go up or down in answer and it would give an inhuman laugh. Once, he raised his matchete with such vehemence, the thing began to cry.

The dibia said "*Lee anya, mgbe arusi ghoro onye di oke ike ma dikwa mpako anyii na-agwa ya osisi o bu si na ya puta.* Answer me". And it did. I was clear. I took my oath and got the job.

This one was different. There were certificates and pictures on the wall. He had schooled at Yale University, had gone on an European tour, had met Frank Steinmeier back when he was under-secretary of state. I reminded self of photoshop.

His shrine seemed to be in a back-room. The incense wafted in, nothing fetish. He walked into the sitting room with a rolex and an ornate class ring right next to an amulet and a copper wire ring. He felt like faculty.

"So you are the two pilgrims? You there, take this alligator pepper, chew it and spit our to your hands. Use it against your entire face"

I assumed the pose of righteous indignation: face lifted, eyes narrowed and the guttural voice of the offended. "I am a Christian"

He laughed. "So are you but what is Christianity? Take"

"I did not come here for a theological discussion"

"What did you come for?"

I had taken the alligator pepper and methodically rubbed it against my face before I considered my actions. "Do you work for the government?"

He excused the pipe enough to say "No, I do not"

"Who are you?"

"You have been old and now you are young, and you have foreclosed on your identity too often to not require our special attention. Think of it this way: in every young person, there is a time the blanket is removed, security is gone, the identity is shaken and she might make a commitment without exploring alternatives."

"Not for me"

"Ostrich. You knew the new state would repress you and yet you voted for it. That was a commitment without, first, a dedication to nigerian unity. Or a consideration of africanity"

"There were no alternatives"

"There is always one. Self."

"Being selfish is not exactly the way to advance in life."

"True. But you are not meant to advance. This rat-race? Its a mirage. You are in the same place, inside the pot. The man running fiercely and the one still are in the same place. One imagines himself cause and the other effect but it is the same event"

Abbe said "Sounds like you're saying, whats the point in being wise if one ends up the same way as a fool. Ecclasiastes 2:15?"

"Yes. And the answer is in the sixteenth so often wrongly translated. *For there is no remembrance of the wise man even as of the fool forever, seeing that in the coming days, all is forgotten,* all heroism and success is forgotten. *And how shall the wise die with the fool?* the righteous prosper their children, prosper in their deaths"

"So man should stop running? All social advance would cease?"

"No. Just the misery. Point me the man who has come upon an epiphany in race. It is the quiet outcast, the silent spirit, the archimedes bath to which society owes its advance"

I kept quiet. There is the confidence of a man aware of next speech and this man without a name was a grandmaster with the patient humour of single-digit checkmate. I kept quiet because yes, I had known I would support self-determination and fail to obtain any. Self would not have led me wrong in that case.

Abbe said, in casual reverence "You know the bible?"

"The difference between Priest and Academic is no different than fox and hedgehog" The man said.

Abbe turned to me slapped his thigh in surprise "Did you

hear that. How do you know Isaiah Berlin*"

"So man must be one or the other?" I asked.

"Thats why we are discussing Identity. There is a stage of diffusion, you do not go outside and you not stay inside with reason. That's where you are stuck. An avoidance of society and rejection of self. "

"I dont avoid society" I really did not, I tell you. I had evening students each weekday and a baby coming.

"But you dont accept self, yes? He laughed. "But what then is your identity?"

"Christian. Lecturer. A man getting along well in tough circumstances" I had the words now

"And you were always a christian? always a teacher? Always bound by circumstance?"

"Okay, okay" What was his name. "enough with the parables"

"That is all words are. But luckily, this is no therapy session. You can see things for yourself"

"You mean Hynopsis?" I asked.

"God, no. A restful walk in the garden, brief stay outside the pot"

"Wait. You wish to put me in some altered state to discover this your morbid truth"

"Yes. Because they called for you"

Mad men are proud, I tell you. Perhaps each one considers himself a genius. I laughed. "Why?"

"You do not know who you are"

"Very. Insightful." Was this what it took? Inherited wealth and insanity enough to prophesy to strangers. I looked at Abbe. Curiosity had been satisfied.

"Abikú must live for God and self but you have always been the loyal servant. They said you should begin now before wa or poverty teaches you. Are you not tired of the sea?"

"Very. Original. Now, dear Delphi..." I drained the tea.

"I have an early day tomorrow so thank you."

"Dada, the best Generals recieve their commission and afterwards disdain any other authority while in the field. Do not wait for the war before you announce self"

Full-blown psychosis. His name, his name, but I found myself saying "My name is not Dada but sure, I'll announce self tomorrow. Thank you so much"

I thought I had risen. "And these are the powers of Paga...the powers of African Traditional Religion, holding me here?"

"African Traditional Religion is a mouthful, isn't it?" He was grinning like a child "And ATR sounds like an automobile. Paganism is perjorative and native medicine sounds too narrow."

He burst into laughter "You looked like a white man who halts suddenly before the word Nigga falls off a practiced tongue. Why don't we simply call this Secularism, brother?"

"Secularism? That is state power and inclusivity?"

"That too. Secularity does not claim a monopoly on truth. To us, morality is a legacy of all humans, living and dead. Ethics is a function of the tribe and not a revealed scroll. Truth, like white light, is splintered through the environment and ourselves.

"We do not care if you are a deacon in the church and return home to pour libation to your grandfather. We do not preach. No man dies an atheist anyway. It is a live-and-let-live system with equality and personal responsibility."

"And this is Africa's great contribution to mankind? Don't answer that. You talk of the individual one time and tribe the other. Why?"

"Yes, that's why Africa is the Mother. Would you sneer at the Enlightenment? It was Africa's cultural truth, secularism, which passed into Europe as the Enlightenment, as Humanism, around the same time your forebears were happily picking guns and crosses from the coast"

He had a point. "But what about this talk of unity and identity, tribe and self"

"The tribe is a function of self. The individual is fountain of state. If you had a choice, integrity demands you pick what is best for you. The family, village and state benefit from your selfishness"

"And who defends the interests of the state when a group of selves attacks it?"

"Every man and woman because the principles they are defending would be truly theirs. Does this remind you of something"

"Yes, France"

"And America and many a state since"

"And the Reign of Terror"

"No that was because they stopped considering self, first surrendering to Robbespiere and finally to Napoleon the third."

"It is possible but what you are saying..."

"Is that Science was mined from Africa like gold from the ancient rock. There is no book, the truth is in your face and in bones and the words you choose and the thing itself. Truth is different from belief; so your personal deity and household rules do not hold sway against objective truth in the tribe. Your consciousness is lower than objective facts. Does this not remind of you of modern science?"

"It does. It does and this cultural truth is returning to Africa, isn't it? A Great Enchanment, like a pentecostal revival of Juju" I was chuckling. Grabbed my chest.

"Chest pain?"

"Yes. Nothing serious. An old friend since childhood. Go on. Why are you laughing"

He shrugged "Same place you always get stabbed. And your brutus is forever female. At-least cross the rubicon early this time"

It was Abbe's turn for disbelief "So by a miracle he has been returning to earth since roman times"

"I do not know, so far." I snorted.

"Christianity, Judaism and Islam claim miracles. What they mean is Magic, an invisible act of will. Yet both of them deny the other's miracles or claim it is wrought by the respective devils. The Atheist denies Magic although his life runs upon it. The secularist understands that he is the source of the magic, that harmony with his environment enhances it, that he can live his dual existence as day and night.

"So when they build temples and write texts, he builds

shrines and add his soul. That is the difference, sho get? *Orisa nikan ni ogo Olorun.* The Shrine is a portal to God-hood held open by the dead and entered by the living. Like your body. I am an Orisa. We all are."

"I have seen many strange things but I still cannot understand this" Abbe turned to me. *What? The evident lunacy? The conquest of will?*

The man, whose name was an impossible request, responded "We have the knowledge but lack the words. And if I said them, you would doubt them. It is why I will make things easy for us. We pass knowledge how our fathers did, leading you to the entrance of the pot. Outside time, you will know and remember your identity"

"I won't do that"

"They are just dreams, Dada"

"My name is Barinem"

He ignored me "Your dreams are memories. This is no different." He looked wistful "Except that everytime you seek to wake, you will leave that body towards another experience. You will think you have woken up but you are stuck in history, in the past and cannot wake up until by some series of events, you reach me again"

"How long will this take"

"Three days and three nights"

"You must be crazy..."I began, turned to Abbe "Seems its time to go"

"No I'm not. You're safe. I assure you I've done it"

"I would die first before I let you put me under for three days. I don't care if you've done it before, I" I felt the need to pause, to understand the warmth reminding me of childhood.

The man was laughing. Abbe was still looking concerned. I could not tell if he was helpless or compassionate accomplice. The motions were slow, vivid and beautiful. I asked them "What the shrine is so funny?"

"You've already drunk it." They were pointing at the tea the maid had brought in an hour ago. The man was saying "Happy Communion" but it came from far away.

I had played varsity hockey and suffered concussions; my doctor called them the cause of my frequent migraines. Assuming I survived this poison, I did not want another incident; It made me irritable and my students deserved better.

The students! I knelt and lay down gently on the rug. I had to call someone at the university, faculty, somebody. Evening lecturers were being sent away for any cause. I needed this job. My hand went towards my waistpocket.

There was a hand helping. Abbe, rotten batman, telling me not to worry, he would be here, right here. *Was he in on this with this whats-his-name?*

The voice faded and then returned in violent crescendo. It was in my head and the fog was clearing. He would be here. Here.

ABIKU

Wole Soyinka

In vain your bangles cast
Charmed circles at my feet
I am Abiku, calling for the first
and repeated time.

Must I weep for goats and cowries
For palm-oil and sprinkled ash?
Yams do not sprout amulets
to earth Abiku's limb

So when the snail is burnt in his shell,
Whet the heated fragment, brand me
Deeply on the breast -You must know him
When Abiku calls again.

I am the squirrel teeth, cracked
The riddle of the palm; remember
This, and dig me deeper still into
the god's swollen foot,

Once and the repeated time, ageless
Though I puke, and when you pour

Dele Bliss Paago

Libations, each finger points me near
The way I came, where

The ground is wet with mourning
White dew suckles flesh-birds
Evening befriends the spider, trapping
Flies in wine-froth

Night and Abiku sucks the oil
From lamps. Mothers! I'll be the
Suppliant snake coiled on the doorstep
Yours the killing cry

The ripest fruit was saddest
Where I crept, the warmth was cloying.
In silence of webs, Abiku moans, shaping
Mounds from the yolk.

EMPIRE

sum sine regno

ART

T hunderclap.

He should be here. "Here, Eletu. Eletu"

A dream is our moon in lockstep, met halfway and in suffi-cient logic. I remember the pride, I tell you. Eight thousand people were present that harmattan. This was Lagos.

There were Europeans and brown children; guests from the Kingdoms of Dahomey, Benin and Opobo; men from Sokoto, that fabled desert land of the Sultan, a place whispered in fearful disdain like Ivan's Russia -and this would have been sufficient reason for the Eletu's annoyance.

I knew these things purely. One does not discover the start of time within it. I had picked Agbada for wear this morning, had eaten Akara for breakfast, was royal chamberlain, a herald today and had to arrange the procession of guests. Watch the crowd.

I knew the words coming right out my mouth: "Right here. Eletu, *ekabo*, right here."

The Eletu Odibo was not listening. He had decided upon ar-rival that the problem was not the couple seated up the dias with such smug looks.

It was the solemn saharan visage, a fifth column, which he now preceeded to count loudly, stopping at odd numbers to exclaim with disbelief "twenty-nine. Twenty-nine! Inside Lagos! *Ah, Ogun ti fi wa sile o!* Thirty..."

At other times he turned to his entourage to exclaim "do you see this?"

The charade would expand briefly to include other heads shaking and voices piping up a "Eko oni baje" while their patron resumed his count.

The entourage held some fifty people -guards, wards, slaves, children and wives -his entire household, proof of a success unaffected by the cirumstances of this wedding.

He was on a roll with "Thirty-nine. Thirty-Nine! Ah, Ah..." when Jose Franscicos dos Santos interrupted to talk of things best left unsaid.

Santos was portuguese; a short stout man already tanned on Brazilian plantations before his decade-long residence here.

Now he was the sunburnt self-appointed doyen of foreign traders in Lagos distrusted by the Europeans on account of his dark skin and by the Africans on account of his blue eyes.

He was a gifted negotiator, a necessary evil, and he held himself aloof except on nights like this one where a mixture of palm-wine and whiskey made him intolerable.

He lay prostrate before the Eletu Odibo in native greeting and rose up to ask how the Eletu felt about losing the beautiful Arabesola to Kosoko.

The Eletu gave a hollow laugh and said in yoruba "these uncooked children have no manners". The entourage laughed on cue.

"Whom? Kosoko or myself?" was the rejoinder.

"Do I truly need another wife?" Odibo gestured with his staff to his household

"You thought so a month ago. I'm merely curious, caboceer, how it feels to not get your way"

The polite smile of a man wishing to be left alone. "Your curiosity can always be satisfied in council"

He meant the trade council, the informal assembly of chiefs and Europeans, where the market on everything from pepper to bodies was regulated.

The portuguese laughed. "But your highness is not as emotional about money as he is about love."

"We are Africans, Jose. We do not love"

"Oh but every society passes that stage. First, the political marriage. Then the commercial. And finally, the amorous"

The Eletu snorted "I was just counting the Muslims here, strangers like yourself. It is a foolish man who goes to another man's house and seeks to rearrange the furniture. A blight. Both of you"

"Hardly. It should be our pride that the hands of our Oba reach so far and wide that the Muslims serve him gladly and the Europeans pay tribute to his son the prince. Would his highness disagree?" It was my voice. I, Dada, royal chamberlain.

The Eletu turned to me in mockery " Would his highness agree? This is the decay I am pointing out. A slave speaking to me, the Eletu Odibo?" His fly-whisk moved. Dismissal.

The Eletu Odibo was not that important. He was first among the Akarigbere chiefs who chose the Oba, a kitchen cabinet. He was a ceremonial prime minister with the power to install but not depose, to advise but not create policy. I could hold a wry smile and did.

The kingmakers inherited their role but elected the Eletu for a lifetime. In these times, they had chosen an ambitious man fascinated by Westminster. A populist demagogue with the self-appointed mandate to rescue these feudal lords from the growing powers of the Palace. Good-luck.

He was right about one thing. Lagos was changing, I tell you. It had been an insignificant outpost of the Benin Empire and its eight ruling families were direct descendants of the first imperial commanders -an imposition on the natives, the Awori and Isheri.

Now we knew the cities and politics of Europe. I and the bridegroom had schooled at the academy in Bahia. We went often as tourists to the cape of Good Hope, for the air and the dutch women.

The Oba entertained Islamic scholars at the Iga Idunganran. Lagos was changing and with it the importance of a fly-whisk.

1496 and the Europeans had come in large numbers seeking slaves. Lagos became an international port paying tribute to Benin. 1700 and the annual slave trade grew to two million bodies. It was good business. The first days of foreign investment.

And we had the advantage of the lagoon. It moved canoes and foodstuff, ivory and textile, manillas, pepper, spies and credit between the Allada and Benin Empires, the Ijebu state and Oyo's southern port.

Soon we had more immigrants than indigenes and were conducting open-air sales. The lagoon had traffic jams and a toll-gate. There was a Trans-Atlantic ship to Bahia every Friday. The ticket office was a crowded affair. Crude adverts lined the market; Go see the world and return with a saunter.

The day came when the Oyo Empire collapsed. Ibadan, Ijaye and Abeokuta claimed her heritage. We wanted ours. We gave credit and lend-lease agreements for the wars which now broke out like forest fires.

There was warehousing for the slaves captured, guarantees for the ownership of lands and the security of property, a small expeditionary force for the sake of balance of power, you see.

We slept an outpost and woke up hosting a standing army, building a navy, needing a bureaucracy. If the Oba still sent tribute to Benin, it was only an insurance policy against local intrigues.

The palace held some 14,000 pounds each year, from tax and tribute and trade. It housed a thousand royal servants, commanded some five thousand men armed with turkish scimitars and european pistols.

There was a six-hundred boat navy to police the lagoon and hold government shares in slave enterprises. We owned three transatlantic ships outright. The wealth of all nobles were dependent on the pensions and privileges tied to the palace; these akrigbere barons had become a cabinet.

I gave the smile and said "Ah, but I am not just any slave, your Highness. I am the royal chamberlain"

Chief of Staff. In the absence of the royal family, in the interregnum, it was I holding court with foreign dignitaries and settling local trade disputes. I could commandeer half the armed men in his entourage and if I exulted in these crumbs of power, it was because 'slave' had been spit into my face all my life.

I was born a Tiv prince, captured in my teens during the Lagos incursions into my native land. They brought me here in chains, the King's loot to sell or gift or keep.

I did not kneel -horsehides would not make me, threats did not serve -and the King paired me with his second son. He made me family, a freeman, but no African society forgets your dawn.

The Eletu was a stout man with a large head and character

untouched by the African Aphrodite, Osun. In anger, he acquired an extraordinary ugliness quite useful in wrestling days. The opponent would ponder the repulsive sight and soon lose ground. I had seen it too often to buy the trick.

"*Akindanidani! Wo eleyi Alainiran. Ati okowa baleje Oloriburuku. Didinrin yii ba mi soro. Ohun ti n sele si eko*"

"Eletu"

"*Dakeje ki n to lu o*" Shut up before I slap you. I laughed. Impotent rage carries the wildest imagination. The Eletu Odibo looked apoplectic.

"Better not let my father hear you" Opolu said soon as his mouth re-opened.

She had come up to this drama, smile playing at the edge of her lips. *Ori ote* Lips taut with royal reticence, the *atike* an artful glow, the tattoos precise and delicate.

"Your Majesty" he spat. We three bowed and the entourage knelt or prostrated.

"Your Highness. I believe the ceremony is about to begin" and she stared at me as she turned away.

I and the princess had a signal for private discourse. It was rarely used. Eyes were sufficent speech.

Opolu was the second richest person in the kingdom with some three thousand slaves and four hundred boats, some of them war-canoes.

She could not inherit the crown and what a pity. She had turned the hereditary intellect -that true divine right -into commerce and amassed lands, slaves, servants and ships second only to the King's.

People said her spirit was male or that of an ancient long-menopausal witch; that she was dominant and a woman should not be so; that she ate babies.

But she was a little girl in my presence. Soft, slender and incredibly seductive, thirty-three and content in the throes of a childhood crush.

Kosoko and I schooled far away. A different continent. Idewu the first son was resident at the bini court of Oba Ewuare and Opolu had been kept at her father's side.

The other fourteen siblings roamed Badagry and Epe, Oyo and Sokoto but once a year, at the yam harvest, we would all gather again.

Kosoko and I would take turns in the captain's cabin, directing the sailors with celestial navigation. There never was a day our ship would dock and the girl in a red dress and ring of attendants would not be waiting.

She would mock our skills if we were a day late, pretend prescience if we were a day early. She would call her elder brother *Oko mi*. My Husband. She would have no words for me, merely a stare. I was Dada Anthonio and a look.

When she stared at me, I quietly retired -we had a spot between the palace walls, a small guardsroom and I held its only keys. It was connected through heavy oak doors into the underground passageway leading into the King's private quarters.

Her own quarters were the next. She had access to the King's private study where the brick-walls, Lagos had brick-walls now, so cleverly overlapped that they were invisible unless one sat at the desk.

She went through her route and I went through mine and there we were, groaning and asweat when the King died.

But for the death, my absence was nothing strange. I was royal chamberlain and a master of the wedding ceremony but still only a foil.

The bride's family produces the second herald whose warrant was to insult the first, praise the bride, chide the groom, and cajole the audience into giving gifts -all done with a background of music for politeness.

A man marries an entire family and the village should dicover his lot in the herald elected among its buffonish young as representative.

I had done all the procession work the day before. I had delegates out there. Besides, custom insists I attend the princess at her order.

Opolu wanted to reward me. My direct reprimand of the Eletu Odibo was unspoken policy. The royal house had suffered from the arrogance of the Akarigbere class of chiefs. But Lagos was changing and now we could insist upon royal prerogative.

To be publicly reminded of his newfound insignificance, at an event already an insult, was statecraft although I enjoyed it. Happiness is politics.

Kosoko had taken Arabesola, bethrothed to the Eletu, and there they were, beautiful in gold lace, getting married. Our native Achilles would hang if absent.

He did not, could not, speak treason and as we stood there, me in humble pose while the other hurled invectives, pissed upon my family tree and spit over the restraining hands of his entourage -all knew where true power lay.

Opolu spoke, smiled in her thoughtful fading way, stared. I entered the guardroom as the great horn sounded.

The other master of ceremony could handle things. At his order, the drummers would rally, the crowd would part and the lines would fall together. The procession would begin.

First would come the royal family; a small clan befitting a prosperous Oba. The royal immediate and another twenty-three wives with their children. The living wives of his father, the wards and guards of the palace. Then the chiefs, each in his class, with his colour and household.

The outsiders would come next. The Dahomey delegation, the sullen Bini representatives, servants of the sokoto potentate, the Calabar merchants, and finally the European traders behind Santos.

The rain made the last few hurry. This was harmattan. It came unprovoked, unannounced, poor omen for a ceremony bound by nature and priests into dryness. The Europeans had not reached their chairs and huddled beneath a boabab.

This was harmattan. Someone must have made it rain. The Priests and Levites, *Ifa* and the *Ogalade*, rose with importance and began incantations.

"Oh its nothing to worry about" Jose told new Europeans "You see that certain of the *Ogalade* have risen up to gather around their leader? They are offering prayers and the rain will stop"

It stopped as suddenly as it came and Jose nodded intensely at each one who cared to look at him as if to say "You see?"But he did not enjoy this attention long.

The sleet had vent its last fury on a horizontal blast against the dais, wetting royal fronts like light sweat, enough to force eyes shut and cause a violent shiver but certainly not enough, one must blame juju, for what happened next.

Oba Osinlokun seemed to forget how to breath, grasped his chest, seemed to stand as though propelled by some ghost, and seemed to crumble.

I hear the royal servants had shielded his Majesty at the start of this drama such that one could not be sure what had happened.

The Princes, one a groom and the other obligated, could not leave the dais. I heard the whistle and went outside the guard-room to find the palace in disarray as servants checked for the royal chamberlain.

I saw the King. I spoke to his personal babalawo. I lied to the servants. I sent a message to Opolu who was certainly not on her seat but was found reading in her quarters.

Afterwards, I went out to the people and with tremendous composure announced that the King, exhausted by the people's goodwill sought a rest and had commanded the feast to continue under the guidance of his eldest son.

He was certainly on the threshold of death. He would not last the night. But art had to go on. It was a statement I and Opolu agreed upon. Who would broadcast such omens on Kosoko's wedding?

As Chamberlain, I would govern administrative matters on my own discretion until a new Oba was selected. My first orders were to send out earthen pots of palmwine and casks of whiskey; drown the people in amnesia, push the owanbe into the next noon.

Officially, the Oba died three days later. A good omen. Yes, he had held death at bay to see the prince marry and now he had gone to the spirit world to be sired anew by his favourite.

The people agreed. The burial was a celebration and added a week to the wedding feast. I sent out more alcohol, hired profes-sional mourners from among the wedding dancers, gave the city the traditional holiday and feast.

Fine art, given the circumstances. And we thought we had done well.

Rarely is the long hand of fate and the short ones of human will extended upon the same time and place but with the sudden illness of Osinlokun and the stubborness of a marriage, Lagos entered its decline that moon-lit night of 1837.

I remember we walked by the Lagoon that night after his eyes closed. She cried softly into my danshiki, aware of death in a way few people are until they meet it, then wiped her tears and assured herself that after all, it was the way of all men or something similar, only to be struck again by another fond memory and the impossibility of more into more tears.

I was merely ashamed that my benefactor had died and his spirit, which in his first moments of disorientation, would stumble through the walls and people of his household, found me *sun pelu omobinrin re* on his son's wedding day. Any day was bad enough.

She was pregnant. My child. Her eyes were wanting. *Would he come to us?* I did not know. We walked by the Lagoon that night and it was the last moment of peace.

1837

Oba Osinlokun, *Oba paapaa ni iku*, four hundred and first Orisha, the visage of the Gods, *Kabiyesi o*.

Kabiyesi, hear the living. Answer us from *Iboji*. Osinlokun! Osinlokun O! Was 1837 not a bad year for death?

By 1837, the civilized world had decided war between them or against America was too costly; the greatest sport could be exported to Asia and Africa.

It was agreed arguments at the Rhine were well-traversed and far too disruptive; helped that Africa did not have a map. Governments could argue of the Nile or Niger without the fatigue of citizenry or boredom of soldiers.

There was William the Comet and Queen Victoria ascended her throne about the same time Louise Phillip I of France arrived the scene.

The youthful duo would replace the declining powers of Denmark, Spain and Portugal. A new age as infantilizing as it was enlightening for Africa would begin.

These were times of maternal concern on all thingsdomestic and foreign, temporal and spiritual.

There were the Opium wars, the South Australia Act, The Government of India Act, The Slavery Abolition Act, The Marriage Act such that the English Parliament may have legislated upon heaven itself if it had considered the industrial weather inclement.

There were Egyptians in Acre on concerns of Ottoman expansion. The Russians were in India and Warsaw. There was Charles Darwin on the Galapagos Island and the Americans were in Mexico. The French Foreign Legion was created to be in every corner of the planet beginning with Algeria.

A cholera epidemic followed these adventures. It reached Moscow from India, touched Poland, swept France, ravaged London and Canada, entered New York. Baptist preachers called it the hand of God against busybodies.

But it was an inconstant hand. If some things broke, others came together. These were the years of the second French revolution, of the Trail of Tears, of Trans-Atlantic steamboats and the Book of Mormon -rosy roads of grief.

The Greeks recieved liberty. The territory of winsconsin was created around the same time Egba refugees founded Abeokuta.

And technology gathered pace. The Colt revolver and the Daguerre Camera were invented in pursuit of the finalities of memory.

The telegraph was built and Babbage began his work on an analytical engine. There were railroads now crisscrossing the United states and continental europe.

It was the age of the commons. Dickens and Hugo held sway across the Channel, writing the mass of mankind formerly invisible. There was Wordsworth and Gerard de Nerval; Lord Bryon. Mikhail Lermontov. Herman Melville.

Carl von Clausewitz considered war and it is no coincidence that the Divine changes tribe -Isreali, Roman, Arabian, English- right when he is known well enough for a treatise.

But the living arts flowered too. There was Wagner and Guiseppe Verdi; Lincoln in springfield.

It was the last days of international flesh. Cinque -a prince like me pressed into unjust slavery -had led a rebellion aboard the Spanish HMS Amistad.

His African colleagues along the slave-coast led rebellions against the abolition of slavery, raised a call for a new economic order free of gun-boat diplomats.

They were called immoral by pauline European powers who had seen the light after four centuries of the trade.

They needed salvation, Europe said. And salvation needed a navy to force freedom, a police to ensure peace within such freedom, then government because the police had to be watched and tax for the watching. Colonialism was born.

The Gods render us their plaything, the prophets a line of officers. But Oba Osinlokun, you who talks with the Orishas and holds death in a calabash, *ma paro fun mi*, 1837 was a poor year to die.

Lagos was steering, from lagoon into the sea, outpost to international port, and needed steady hands.

The death of the monarch was accompanied by that suspicion, false bonhomie, and encounters in dark corridors which hurry the departure of all men of property. The state foundered.

The seven Kingmakers received three hundred pounds each, ten slaves and an emissary from Adele, brother of the dead king, on the understanding that they would remind the Ifa oracle of a certain exile.

The cabociers expressed their fervent well-wishes and gratitude through the emissary and informed the Badagry exile that Orunmila was sole controller of his divine Oracle. Pray.

But there was a peculiar meeting at the port where European traders sought assurances from the Eletu Odibo and other chiefs. It was held at the tavern, in daylight; nothing to see beyond a friendly exchange of views between business associates.

Jacques the French was responding to the Priest and his assertion of Pax Britannica "English pride is not lost on this one"

"The French envy us" and the priest winked at Odibo

"No, the French pity you. We have colonies from the Algiers to the Americas to Africa. What have you?"

"The authority of the seas. The authority to abolish slave trade and force all the continental powers to follow suit. We have not imposed ourselves anywhere but on the side of truth and liberty"

"Oh but there is something Father Thomas fails to mention" said Theodore. "And perhaps it is the most important of all. The convulsions of government on the continent have never reached England. We have the most stable society of all"

"Not for long. Your Prime Minister, he was forced by circumstances to serve a woman. We here are more stable than you. Here the Prime Minister chooses and the state cannot be in female hands" The Eletu said.

The frenchman had no love of diplomacy "No, Eletu, do not compare yourself to the Viscount. Here you are the Kingmaker and afterwards you make no policy. In London, Lamb was made by the King, then the Queen and afterwards he makes the policy."

Captain Theodore called it beside the point "The yoruba have not had enough time, no offense Eletu. The ideal style for a people is to preserve the institutions of the past, merely changing them insensibly and little by little to fit the present. This ideal is difficult to realize and takes a long history. The romans in ancient and the English in modern times are almost alone in having realized it"

Here Father Thomas piped up the clerical: "I say alone. Nothing 'almost' about the fact that we, as our institutions and language, and religion too, have evolved into the manliest version humans know."

"Even Africans see the difference between the graceful reserve of the English, the general excitability of other Europeans, especially Latins, and their own savagery on this continent. Thank the Almighty for Pax Britannica. Benevolent father is what we are, in the footsteps of Christ, civilizing the world, each thing permitted to evolve with the least trouble, in peace, and we only come in like the gardener to prune this branch and that."

"Don't you see how Britain, the most democratic society in the world, is a monarchy? But whenever a state calls itself a republic, it certainly is run by a concealed despot or a cabal. We have mastered Human Nature"

Jacques laughed. "The fanatic cannot be saved. *Le temps de L'ile affecte certainement la sante mentale*. It must be a burden to go everywhere with the assurance of a benefactor and find yourself despised for no apparent reason".

Father Thomas, his face grown red from the flush of alcohol, looked ready to announce another homily.

The Eletu spoke."Mr French, They are not despised here. Mr English, this is not a savage land. Do you not see that we have the same institutions?"

At disbelief, the Eletu turned to Chief Etu and said "They think they know us because we have given them land by the sea"

"We have laws, embassies, police. Our chiefs are parliament and have you not heard of Adele whom I removed from office for insulting such institution?" It was an exaggeration but let us forgive a drunk man.

This was an opening. "Whatever the merits of your laws and systems, I must say it suffers shames whenever the King arbitrarily raises taxes against the wishes of the Parliament you speak of" Jacques said.

"Rump Parliament" Captain Theodore said

"Your parliament votes at the King's pleasure and it laws can be easily set aside by royal prerogative. Well. It is a start, your sort of Magna Carta"

Josef the Dutch refused. "No it would not be their charter moment. The estates are still all bark and no bite"

"The tax raise was a one-time thing. I can assure you gentlemen..."

"What sort of Prime Minister are you, Odibo, if you do not know taxes are yeast"

The Eletu stared at the irreverent french, a notorious tide gathering. Jacques showed tobacco-teeth "Is this how you treat your friends? We hear it will be increased again"

"Never! We have very clear understandings with the new soveriegn"

"Who did you choose?"

The Eletu was back to bonhomie "The Gods, not I."

"Who?" The Priest pressed

"Order more drinks for this trade union." Another laugh. Odibo turned to Chief Abiade "They wish to influence state affairs and yet give nothing"

I heard of this meeting and only remember it because the historian points to this cause or that when we know the rise and fall of empires are due to words said upon alcohol.

They drank into the night, trading gifts, discussing the impossibility of upsetting tradition so by the involvement of every sort of blood in governance. The important part had been settled.

A DEMOCRAT

Ipebi. Idewu spent three months learning the sacred rites and absorbing the Orishas. Then Oba Idewu, father of the people, orisha on earth, came out to hold the royal staff and sit on the throne. There was a feast.

It was considered poor taste, after announcing itself an empire, for Idewu to pay the customary visit, accompanied by his father's head, to the overlord in Benin City. On this point, all lagosians agreed: they were vassals no more.

Eko was no more a war-camp but a citadel. It's people had drunk palmwine in dionysian fashion the night Osinlokun was buried, head and all, in the newly created royal cemetery beside the Ifa compound.

He was buried in a new style crafted by The Royal council. A tomb the height of a man was built and filled with ivory, silver and slaves. A thatched shrine leaned upon one of its square walls. Engraved on the other three sides were his titles. One had to be careful of precedence.

People died from the alcohol. Slaves died -which is not the same thing. Strung inside the fetid pits because interior traders could not sell captives during festivities and could not trade for space and could not find returning boatsmen. Some seventy slaves died in those twenty-one days -a loss of life and money.

Not that the people minded. There had been seven days of feast after the wedding, another seven for the burial, and a third for the ascension. What was lost in trade was suitably recompensed by the free alcohol, excessive food and the good feeling of striking a bargain in one's favor.

But such things are inconsequential to statecraft. Oba Idewu re-appointed me royal chamberlain and announced his policy.

It was an extension of his father's; subjugate Badagry, Abeokuta and make Lagos the greatest yoruba nation. He laughed at Ibadan and Ijaiye who did not realize they were dependent upon his goodwill. He made a joke about Benin.

Benin responded in a fortnight with seventy envoys who came politely to ask if Lagos wanted war. The people gathered.

The Oba assured the envoys it had been a stupid joke for public consumption. The royal council convinced Benin it would obtain nothing beyond mutual respect. *An alliance sometime in the future, perhaps?* There would be no battle of Thermopylae.

His independence accepted, Idewu now turned to the domestic affairs of the new empire and soon discovered the need for another liberty.

He had solemnly swore "no more taxes" to the Akarigbere, he had assured the kingmakers he would rule-in-council, that he was committed to free trade with the europeans and tough protections against the Fulanis.

But private honour must be trumped by public facts. The British Squadrons had reduced slave sales by seven percent each year since 1935 and the Palace had given too many concessions to steal market-share from Porto-Novo.

The tax commissioner informed the Oba there was some sixty-something percent of revenue outside the tax system because of concessions to the expatriates and privileges granted the most influential caboceers.

Osinlokun's tax-raise had provoked the hiding of profits. There was corruption at the lagoon's toll-gates and at the sea-port. There was a new trade booming, rubber and oil plantations in Abeokuta, and the palace was recieving next to nothing for it.

The Balogun, his War-Chief, announced that the army, two parts being slaves and ineligible for compensation, had yet to pay salaries to the third.

There were public works already in swing, the maintenance of the navy, the large domestic concern of the palace, the mercenary force useful for foreign policy and plausible deniability - the treasury was full and bleeding.

He called a full council meeting. It was an unusual affair so soon after a coronation. The Akarigbere was often sufficient and a full council happened only at traditional events but Idewu was a democrat.

The Eletu Odibo led the Akarigbere -legislative and administrative -chiefs: Eletu Iwashe of the Treasury; Eletu Ika of Justice; Ologun Agbaje, Trade; Eletu Awo, Foreign Affairs. The Ologun Adodo, Ologun Atebo, Ologun Agan, Ologun Igbesodi, Ologun Ide Okoro.

With a full council, the Asogbon was there too, a blatantly black man with face set in perpetual grimace. He led the Agbogbon chieftancy class -the thirty-two commanders of military nobility.

The combined hundred and five chiefs of the Idejo and Ogalade classes -descendants of the first settlers and of the earliest native priests sat in a horse-shoe against the walls of the court-hall.

The Akarigbere chiefs were glad to be assembled. It was costing them money to hide profits. One had to accept gifts, then trade such things to the interior and smuggle bags of cowries back to Lagos. *Could the taxes be rescinded?*

To buttress their argument, the Eletu ensured Jose and five dubious trade representatives of European nations were present at the hour to inform the King how a tax reduction would boost his treasury.

They also petitioned the removal of a royal monopoly on building ships or owning shares in foreign ones.

The palace owned three ships built in Brazil and had recently acquired two steamboats in addition to its large canoes which served as navy and private corporation. Perhaps in these difficult times, Adewu would like to sell off such liabilities. More money for the treasury.

Jose had his own concerns with the Osinlokun tax regime. "Concessions, your Majesty. You see, we have to bribe the captains of the anti-slavery squadron or else hire better ships and the hands to work them. We have to pay you and your chiefs for the storage facilities or else buy land on which to build them. We have to feed our families and build our property. Anywhere we turn, money is there. That is why we cannot continue to pay the twelve percent. If it is reduced to eight, more trades happen. *Kabiyesi*, upon my honour, you will find an increase in revenue"

He wanted this right away. "I always say, in matters of business, steady hand and speedy legs." Nod. Nod and the five representatives nodded with him.

The council was divided. Wealthy chiefs, Akarigbere and most of the Agbogbon, supported and were accused of bleeding the kingdom for private interest by the Idejo and Agalade.

The caboocers owned the baracoons, the slaves, and shares in the trusted ships. Land was not so rich, the palace kept a ceiling on commodity prices. "Loan-shark, Thief, Traitor".

Idewu turned this way and that in earnest imitation of his Father's habit of brisk but undivided attention. Finally, he calmed the crowd and announced his policy. "Twenty Percent".

Monarchs, by any name, require time to absorb office. But a palace and the grooming of the Antonines give an advantage. Idewu's voice had already acquired the commanding balsam of authority from Benin and his father. The room went quiet, uncertain if he had thrown question, joke, or insult.

The chiefs and traders turned to Odibo, first in rank among the courtiers, and the Eletu played it safe by answering all possibilities.

He nodded gravely, he chuckled with a brief smile and he bowed. Only upon doing this, the rest of the court following his example, did he ask "Your Majesty, you said?"

Idewu said "Twenty Percent. That will be the tax."

"Twenty percent?" The Eletu asked.

Idewu spoke slowly. "Yes. Lagos needs to expand and I hope you will all do your part."

He spoke to Jose. "Traders, we sell you slaves for fifteen dollars or less, and you sell them in the America's for six times that. At the least. I say that is enough profit. You will pay for the baracoons and the Oba's Tax. I will give concessions as a private gift, not state policy"

"And, my chiefs, I have seen you steal from my father. I know you will steal from me. But, the tax is set and I will call each to account when I so wish. I know you people dash them bodies and they dash you sofas and cutlery and whiskey to avoid the tax."

"In the past two years, Royal revenue has fallen from twelve pounds in the thousands to somewhere above eight. The troubles from Oyo are not yet over. The tribute from Badagry and Abeokuta are still contested. My subjects are still poor and the public projects of the capital remain unfinished. When these things are done, I may reduce the tax".

Idewu announced that henceforth, royal servants -my department -would sign every contract or else it would be void. The same would collect the taxes and inspect cargo and police gifts. The details would be fixed later.

"And I would expect tax from the rubber plantations come harvest season. I assure you I have all your interests at stake and will always listen to your opinions but it is I, the four hundred and first Orisha, who must answer to the Heaven and the ancestors for Eko."

The room rift with dissension a few minutes ago now shook their heads and in different ways, said to the King "You cannot do this".

The Idejo reminded him that agriculture was not as profitable as trading. Estate tax was untraditional.

The Akarigbere reminded him of the importance of oaths and the Ogalade, the Priest-Class, wanted a clear exemption from all taxes.

Twenty percent would mean an increase in tariffs on the lagoon and the Asogbon were concerned, soldiers who supported incomes and the military elite with trading would suffer. They hinted at mutiny.

The Europeans looked decidedly distraught. Father Thomas had assured the Anglican Church, and Theodore the Niger Company, that taxes would be rescinded in a year -"a place for God and trade."

Jacques had drawn on every line of credit to establish his business and pay his portion of the collective bribes. The portuguese discovered they hated Oba Idewu far more than the upstart British.

When a man's eyes widen and his neck is veined, when disgust and anger alternately sharpens the mouth into the contortions of hatred, the animal inside feasts upon its first victim.

The Odibo was a giant of a man, a mammoth of a beast straining to break restraint. The word came with vehemence. "Whelp".

He said other very English things and the Idejo and Ogalade raised an outcry. Imperial perogative could sentence him but Idewu asked the council for a vote on this agent of "Outsiders", an instigator of "palaver" -Eko o Simi it Ada Rafa ati fun". The council 115-30 approved his immediate arrest. Democrat.

SUNSET

The people rioted. We assumed that three weeks of alcohol and a vacation given to reason could be cause and the crowd was sent away with gifts. But they returned everyday, larger and more insistent upon his release.

Nobody particularly loved the Eletu. And even if one notes that inconstancy in most men and in every multitude, the reaction of Lagos was far too turbulent to denounce suspicions of european money.

There was no clear agenda beyond his release. I asked and the old said it was a fight for tradition, the young that it was a revolution -Lagos in its new age required an accountable King. People said his release would create jobs. The Europeans kept mum.

We could have waited. A mob desires nothing more than the savour of a response, an evidence of the impact their undistinguished lives have wrought on history. There is nothing more distasteful, nothing more certain to fuel bloodthirst, than sovereign acquiescence.

We argued against it but Idewu was a good man. A democrat. The Oba appeared before them, and they did not allow him speak. There were no prostrations, no bow and -he would not allow me deploy the palace guards -no whip. After a fortnight and another council meeting, Idewu gave the order for the Eletu's release.

The Eletu rode out of town the next morning. Thge departure was conspicuous, a baggage train two hundred metres long and a fifty-strong escort.

People said he was going on exile. The Palace was sated. It informed the Akarigbere it could choose a replacement. The response from the War-Chief struck us. The Eletu had not gone to Badagry. He had gone to pay homage to Benin.

The empty council chairs were another message. The lesser nobles wanted no proscription from Benin and had conveniently excused themselves to attend to countryside holdings. Caboceers with enough strenght for a siege rudely sent our town-criers away.

The youth watched the highway for the Eletu's arrival, waited with bated breath for the first regicide in living memory.

One could not disperse them without more public outrage. It was a tinderbox, all the more capricious because the people had toasted Idewu a month ago "A good man and a great king"; had gathered in solidarity against the Benin embassy; had heard the reasonable demands of a monarch intent on their well-being.

We were told Benin had hosted the Eletu with naked anticipation. Yes, of course, the young man is a rebel. But you the Eletu can not depose him without admitting Bini suzerainty.

Yes, now you say so but what happens afterward? Tyrant follows tyrant. Would you be willing to quarter a thousand Bini soldiers to prevent any further threats to your life or power?

The Eletu understood any power gained would be temporary if he led the Bini into Lagos. In subsequent conferences, he whittled down the occupation troops to half and insisted they come as an escort for Adele.

For his part, he would return with envoys of the King bearing goodwill gifts to the chiefs and heads of households.

He would bear the calabash of poison, the symbol of rejection by people and Gods, meant for Idewu. But he was only the humble Minister of both Lagos and Benin. Let the new King pledge allegiance.

With these terms, the Eletu set out for Lagos. As word spread in the city of bini assent, Eko fell into worse silence. The feasts were over but business remained stalled and the residents walked the streets without looking another in the eye.

That he arrived safe was a miracle. Mercenaries attacked the convoy in Idanre. The arrival of the baggage train bulging with gifts and slaves and guards did not significantly alter equations but it convinced the hirelings that the Bini had sent reinforcements and they rode off into the dawn with as much loot as they could manage. That was the report they gave the palace. Mercenaries.

The attack gave the Eletu a halo. As disguise and statecraft, he wore the ensemble of a Ifa Priest and rode in a small band just after the baggage train.

In Lagos, the elders said the Gods were against Idewu. At Ikole, one of the camp prostitutes was caught putting a cobra in the hut reserved for the Eletu. Her hands were cut off and she was sent ahead to announce his divine arrival.

So great was the crowd of the highway that the party descended from their horses and began to plow through the people, flanked by guards.

The city-square bristled at the bounds and held a buzzing of respectful gossip. The Eletu walked into the palace, Iga Idunganran, shouting as he went: *Ododo ti de.*

The city gates had to be shut for the sacred moment but I placed guards, slaves and horses at the ready for a spirited escape plan. We sat in Idewu's private quarters and considered options again. The dawn itself seemed hesitant.

He sat despondent on his basket chair, flanked by his siblings, and the few loyal remains of his government -myself, the Eletu Iwashe,Oshodi Tapa. *What to do with the Calabash.*

The Calabash was an object and institution intended to hold the Oba in check. A sovereign repulsive to his people would be presented with sword and calabash with a skull. War or Poison. Fight or Die.

For a vassal-state like Lagos -we had dispensed with any delusions of imperial grandeur at this point -the Overlord was Vox Dei est Vox Populis. The request of the Eletu was sufficient.

"The devil and the blue sea" Kosoko had said days ago.

Some of the family, buoyed on by Opolu, advocated the devil on the sound logic that one could conquer beings but nature was too wide, too wild, an attempt.

"We can't, this, all of this, would not be permitted if Baba was standing where you are. *Baba ko ni je ki eyi sele. Je Oba, arankunrin mi olufe!* Is it a secret Benin is afraid of us? *Won ko le kede ogun lati igba naa?* All these years since Baba stopped the tribute? Now they talk of war because they have the traitor. We have Dahomey"

Idewu took time off reflections of his misery to note wryly that his sister should have been a man.

Kosoko snickered "Baba would have made her King"

"Not a bad choice in hindsight". The brothers laughed. We had travelled the world together, I and Kosoko, but our friendship was secondary to the easy camaderie he shared with his elder brother. In turn, Idewu leaned upon his counsel.

"What do we do?" The Oba asked.

"*A nilo akoko*". It was true. The palace needed time to wrest control the army, diversify its wealth, build alliances if it was going to face the Benin Empire, a six-century old behemoth in agonizingly slow decline. Buying time meant Idewu's suicide.

"We could run, brother. Dada has arranged things. Build a government in Epe or Badagry. But that is what they want us to do. *Akii gba eni to yo be mu*. They want to uproot the entire Kutere lineage. *Alantakun bi yoo ba o ja, a ta ka o lara.*"

Opolu would not have it. She turned to Kosoko "*Oko mi*, I have never considered you a coward. What is wrong with all of you. To the west is a powerful empire. To the east another. Dahomey would find reason for common-cause. *Akii fi ti ju karun*"

Kosoko asked Opolu "Common-cause against Benin? Be reasonable, sister. They will slaughter the few of us and easily find replacements for the entire army, even if from just the Oba's house." The room sniggered.

The Oba of Benin, like the king of Dahomey, had alot of women. Three thousand or thereabouts. One cannot say how the government was run if the Oba avidly planted, or if all that sprouted was his, but his children alone were several enough for the Lagos army.

"Your Majesty, plead your case to the Oba of Benin. We can escape tonight" The Eletu Iwase suggested. His presence was resented because he kept a foot in a both camps. His counsel was the detritus of centrist politics.

I spoke. "You are still talking this rubbish? The entire chiefs have denounced him in Benin, they have sent the calabash and he should go there for a public execution?"

"Ah, *mase kegan mi o*. Surely the Oba will respect his prince. *Imoran nikan ni mo fun*. They still need legitimacy here."

"A legitimacy that can be obtained from any of my uncles" Idewu said.

"Akintola does not want the throne. I can swear to Ogun" Odunsi said. "And wherever you go, we follow" His fifteen siblings nodded. Akinsanya shouted "Kabiyesi ooo"

"Oh, *dake.* What of Adele in Badagry?" Oba Idewu turned to me "Dada, *iwo ko so fun won pe o fi awon ebun ranse?* You did not tell them. Plenty gifts. You think he does not want the throne back?"

The Eletu Iwashe thought for a moment "He can be handled in the days between here and Benin"

"*Iwo yoo fe iyen.* So you want an Oba without an army and popular support killing his uncle then announcing himself vassal to Benin and returning to his palace to find what? *Ko ni si alaafia*" Kosoko turned to Idewu "*Nje ohun ti bab yoo ti se?*"

Kosoko was earnest. It is a fine sport to watch saints in their first days. Afterwards they must become hypocrites or lay aside the cassock.

"Calm down, the lot of you" Oba Idewu said.

Opolu laughed a little bit too long in the manner of a sarcast. "The King has no worries. Surely the end of his reign does not stare us all in the face"

"What would you have me do, Opolu?"

"What would I have you do? As if you would take my advice. *Osun kilode ti o fi beere mi?*" Her constant refrain. Why am I female?

"We will hear you if you will speak"

"I will speak, Kabiyesi. Very clearly, by *Mawu.* Is this not *Eko?* Did our ancestors not build this land? Why should the Oba of Benin remove the Oba of Lagos at a whim? *Tani o ni ile yi*"

"You want to fight Benin"

"Why not?"

"You want to fight Benin with all the war-chiefs here on their side."

"Why not? We have enough slaves"

"No sister. No, don't talk nonsense. With all our army, we cannot field twelve thousand men. Benin will bring thirty thousand and it will only be the beginning, Ogun help us if they levy Sapele and Abraka and every other colony."

"Dahomey" When she was exasperated, Opolu would press the back of a palm against her head and sigh a word into existence. She rose up and paced the room that way. She looked tired, fearful, beautiful.

I said simply "Gezo will take all our money and send five thousand men who shout better than they fight."

It was becoming clear to everyone that suicide was the only way to survive this. Dahomey had fought off Oyo suzerainty but would impose theirs upon us. Whatever the Bini court was, it had an easy hand.

"Or send us women" The brothers laughed. The minons of Dahomey were the talk of the sahel and savanna.

She-devils released by Shaitan, an Arabic scholar told us. Amazons, the Europeans called them. for us, It was a joke to think of women in armor, phalanx and war.

Idewu had decided. "Opolu, there is no way out of this. Let us not pretend we have any options in this affair. I should not have released Odibo but now what can we do?"

"You do not understand. This is not only about you..."

"I understand too well, sister. The Eletu wants to be the most powerful man in Lagos. What I understand now, and you seem not to, is that there is no other way to win this man today. You all and Kosoko must do the work."

He rose up and cradled her face. *"Emi ati baba yoo bojuto gbogbo yin.* I will always be here"

"Idewu..." Opolu was at the brink of tears. *"Arakunrin Olufe"* she made a motion at her waist, against the bulge of her wrapper and beads, as though she were pushing grief down to the earth, refusing the rising reaper.

"Easy, sister. Obatala was meant to sleep and Oduduwa to create the world" He nodded to me "Take care of her. Call them in"

I went out to inform the deputation that the Oba was finished with his ancestral sacrifice. Opolu had run out, her face a stoic blanket of grief.

The chiefs had left and so had the young or female siblings. Kosoko, Odunsi, Akinmosa, Adeniyi and the intrepid Oba remained. I joined them.

The Eletu and two Akarigbere caboceers entered with sword and calabash."Well..." the Eletu began.

"You will spare me the torment, Eletu. *Okunrin ti n ku kuku dake*, not the nightmare of your self-importance" Idewu waved to the Chief with the calabash. He drank.

"My will is that my brother ascends the throne. The royal properties remain whole" He drank.

The Eletu said "It shall be done if the Gods will it". We understood the Gods had not willed it.

"It must be painful that you cannot have the crown to yourself. At the height of your power, you still cannot seat here."

"I have never desired the throne, your Majesty. It is a pity you have to leave it this way" There was nothing offensive in the Eletu's behaviour; nothing one could point, no smug look on his face or sotto voce. He probably considered himself a righteous victim.

There was a muffled cry from Idewu as he felt the poison working its way towards its heart. The calabash was never meant as euthanasia.

"Well, I cannot be so kind, Eletu. Ogun curse you. Ki awon olorun bu o. Je ki won ko o, ko ile yii sile titi awon olufowosi re yoo fi pe loni. Then let the earth reject your body. Into the lagoon, into the lagoon..."

There was a loud shout as the King collapsed, this from the women outside. They would be untying head wrappers and participating in the traditional choreography of grief.

We stood until the Eletu Odibo, satisfied, left the room. Then we sat silently, our eyes upon the body and thoughts far away.

That night, three horsemen set out for Badagry with an urgent message for a certain exile. The Eletu had had enough with the house of Osinlokun.

THE INQUISITION

Nobody knew when the Swede met Africa. He sold nothing, owned nothing and slept in the backyard of the Pirate Tavern. He was a little man, immaculately dressed, walking like a shadow inside and around the tavern.

The Priest described the swede's face as "built of little skin and too many muscles". He was not popular. It did not help that his stern visage masked the most pleasant voice.

Men are apt to interpret everything else so; perhaps the obsession with cleanliness masked a familiarity with the sordid.

We say he owned nothing because his was merely the civilized garbage of the homeless. A restored table from the pirate, two suitcases full of books and papers, a box of his clothes always in decently neat form and a military cot said to be stolen from the ship most likely to have brought him. The HMS Phillips.

People said other things. He was a journalist -a catholic priest, an escaped convict, one of those on the know of the Polish assasination, a Russian spy, a nephew to Lord Bryon -on different afternoons.

They spoke of vampires on humid days and asked him of his relationship with Bismarck on mild ones. The women were attracted to him, or rather to the mystery and that voice, and then people said he was one of those Freemasons.

He never went to church. Black people swore they knew the

bible better than the european backslider. To put a hand upon the plow.

But the Swede, who rarely gave his name but answered each inquiry in its native dialect with such a polite and pleasant refusal that one considered it rude to insist, remained an enigma.

A stranger suffers inordinate inquiry, it is true, but the Swede was to blame too. Every month, sometimes more often, a schooner would arrive on the Lagoon with a private bag of letters and a boy; the latter suggested as courier for the things which could not enter paper or perhaps deliver money.

Outside his frenzied walks on such days, he seemed to spend all morning praying, all afternoon singing upon a battered guitar, and all evening getting drunk, seducing women, baffling men and retiring to the backyard -the taut face still avidly animated in sleep.

Then he went on a tour of the shrines in Yoruba-land, a feat that should have rendered him a perverse but equal reputation with Livingstone and Mungo. He said nothing about it.

One morning, the Swede went to the Ifa compound and he was given a hut.Was he an initiate? One of those heretical monks escaping continental Europe?

It was in that hut that Odamola met him. He was something of curiosity, this white man crosslegged on a mat amid *Opele* and *Opon Ifa*.

Africans enjoyed consulting him, not least because he did not charge beyond a token for Dafa. Odamola complained to him of infertility.

First she asked him how an European was finding black Gods. "And have you given up Jehovah"

"Would you give up Olorun? I do not think Gods have any color"

She said she liked his answer or his voice. He did not respond. She told him "I can't have a baby" as she received tea from his hands.

And he touched her shoulder as he told her *"mase paro fun awon orisa"*.

Our samaritan woman stayed until nightfall, relegating every thought of the beating and rape -she called it rape -she would endure that night to the effeminate charm of a hard-boiled Swede.

She informed Oba Adele that she knew just the man to run the Igbakaun Society. She slept in his hut on the off-duty nights.

An Ifa Priest would not marry. they settled into a routine where he provided her with herbs for abortion and healing while she helped him with the moonlit rituals for the Gods.

It was one such night, after her ebony skin was cleansed of chalk and the grass of the clearing and their sweat of their sex, that she mentioned Igbakaun to him. He was quiet a long time.

Adele had returned to the throne mindful of the Eletu. His nephew had been forced to the hemlock for the same reason of his exile two decades ago. Another royal had been executed by council without Ifa.

Clearly the Akarigbere were more confident in the society beneath. The masses would not revolt because of patronage. Another Oba could not amass the sort of power Osinlokun wielded without seeing the strings.

His response was espionage. He would not fight the agreements and piles of concessions upon his desk. He would wait and listen for hubris, feed it even as Kou-Chien.

The palace would launch a civil offensive on its people, adopt a policy of subservience, rebuild its soft power until Wu slipped.

Odamola, an old friend, came with the market women and the King sent me to her with a handwritten note.

I knew nothing else until the swede came to me. She had first spied on her husband for Adele and then suggested the swede as head of secret security for the palace.

That night he said "If your husband finds out, he will kill you" and she cried for this man whose first thought was her welfare.

They did not speak of the matter again but when the King summoned the Swede to the palace, he went through the slave's quarters and through the service door and into the King's bedroom with a plan.

I was called an hour later and informed of my new position as tax inspector. The Eletu had wanted my head long enough.

The Oba could pacify the Akarigbere with my removal, pacify the Idejo with a native vizier and create the Igbakaun under a loyal hand.

I would become a roving tax inspector, recruiting others and advising the swede on palace needs. Operations would remain under his hand. He bought a house from colonel Bircham whose furlough was ended. He bought three slaves and five rifles from the palace.

Afterwards, the swede became choir master of the Aglican Church and a model resident. He maintained residence at the *Ifa* compound, ran *Dafa* on market-days.

But the Bircham place was his country-home, Igbakaun headquarters and he set the rules. No entrance except through the kitchen door. Three knocks with the third long away. Question. Password.

The reports he compiled were the most comprehensive knowledge any African Sovereign could muster. The priests brought news of Gods, yes, but the palace knew which of such priests slept with the vestal virgins and which with wives in the capital and which would spill confessional secrets over what certain quantity of alcohol.

The council stalled the King as he would but slowly he turned the screws. An European trader would call a debt in early, a caboceer would find himself near-destitute, and then the trader would offer a concession "of pity, I assure you mate" to the cabocier for a certain vote on the council.

He would find himself debating the intricacies of white minds while imagining the King as confused about his conversion.

A Chief would find bandits holding half his land at harvest season, a favorite slave with intimate knowledge of the family business suddenly lost, or his son on the slave block and no knowledge of the seller.

He would run to the Palace for royal intervention and find a considerate King already holding mustered troops.

There would be no talk of concessions but the chief understood. As each pair of eyes became clouded with fear and suspicion, the council increased oversight and ordered all taxes paid to the Prime Minister.

In retaliation, the palace bequeathed to the Gods and reduced its slaves from 4,221 to a thousand. Most of those now owned by *Ifa* were the tax collectors. Under authority of the Gods, the priesthood took taxation and policing under its wings.

They maintained the twenty percent rate but of the roughly twelve thousand pounds revenue of 1932, the council saw only two -down from seven thousand three hundred of 1931.

True, they gave the King only a thousand pounds -down from two -but the rest was dedicated to the Gods. The Oba was conveniently an Orisha as well and divine finance crossed eight thousand pounds.

The meetings at the Eletu's House, what they had begun to call parliament, turned feverish.

Two things were certain for the two factions whose tempers rose with every palace manoevuer.

Perhaps we shall them liberals, those men who had begun to wear suits and regimental coats over ankle-length wrapper and asked the Eletu for tougher measures against the King in this new age of Lagos.

The conservatives were sure the King was no more man, that Juju had found home in him, that the other four hundred Orishas were acting as spies and troublemakers and, after they found the body of chief Okule, assasins.

Okule was an old Commander of the army, a veteran of the Ijebu wars when Osinlokun sought to expand Lagos. Already an asogbon chief, he was made a caboceer and given the extreme north of Lagos for a homestead.

When the Muslims began searching for the sea, he was gate-keeper and sudden third wealthiest man. Osinlokun realized his mistake but as Gods do not reverse themselves, the King made Okule a member of council -a promotion that forced the akarig-bere chief and his family to live in the capital.

When the new Minister of War complained of his district turning into ruins, the King granted leave to one family member to return to Ofiza.

The son was burdened with fifteen tax officers, two trade representatives of the palace, and a witch-doctor who kept the willful lad sedated and content.

When the Eletu began his push for more power, Okule whipped Chiefs into the Liberal camps. As court and parliament pulled every ace, Okule played his riskiest yet.

He would order the army at Ijebu, which remained loyal to him, Into the city.The army would demand better salaries, accuse the Ifa of embezzlement, and ask that the council do its job before a starved front would permit the displaced horde from Oyo into the town.

The King and priesthood would agree, Gods or not, because three thousand armed men on palace grounds and in the temple and on the streets would stall libations. That would deter any Orisha from temporal affairs.

The messenger rode off one moonless night but his head was discovered on the sharp bamboo of the Okule Compound. The cabocier decided he was compromised and decided to flee the capital to take command of the army.

The Eletu and the Liberals argued against it. The army could march quick enough with a new despatch and besides the road was rife with gangs pledging allegiance to the palace.

Every new despatch adorned Okule's fence in regular time. Mad with fear one night, the chief grabbed a horse and fled before house guards or family or party could discover his departure.

After three weeks of no news, even the Eletu was sure the old devil had made his way into Ijebu and was returning with deliverance.

The old devil was in a room heavy with the smell of his own shit and piss for those three weeks, very much like the punishment of the ancient Esu by Sango.

The Swede had transformed the dining room into an interrogation room and in that darkness, perhaps he was writer or indigent composer or merely an avid student of the inquisition, art was born.

The twenty-eight day stay of Okule was only the beginning

but it was was lucky in its first subject, confirming a process that would be repeated several times with varied outcomes.

The Swede wrote his impressions in a small red book. When he closed the pages, the body was found on the Eletu Odibo's farmland, almost camouflaged in its green of poison and decay.

News of the death rattled the chieftancy. The conservatives felt themselves absolved of error. The liberals decided it meant war. On the nineteenth of May, 1939, the council opened an investigation into the entire court, from slave to prince. They could not touch the King without *Ifa* support but they could kill every lieutenant.

Seventy-two verdicts of guilt were given, mostly to slaves scapegoated for some absence or unexplained revenue. A few relatives, princes as distant as the twentieth succession, of the ruling house were sanctioned or whipped. It seemed straight from the Eletu playbook: push back but not so hard to lose your balance.

Then when we thought the Terror past its climax, the council called Opolu, Kosoko and myself before them.

The Ogboni insisted the council had the right to summon and sentence any person save the King. We appealed to *Orunmila*.

In a bold move, the Badagry army re-entered Lagos to re-establish headquarters at the *Ifa* compound. The Oracle went silent, which both sides saw as affirmations of suit.

The army kidnapped each of us. The King was unwilling to risk his small force in any confrontation where the *Ifa* Temple had been neutralized. The real trials began.

THE OPOLU PANEL

A woman can bear her name so vehemently it becomes forever male.

Kosoko had appeared contrite, deftly bribing his way into liberty and poverty. I went before them as the messenger in dark, the courtier used for purposes impossible to discern.

I had lied with such consummate skill the Swede, represented in the sessions by a dusty boy of fifteen, sent me his father's ring as a token of respect.

Opolu charged and raved and threatened civil war. Perhaps it was the death of Idewu for she had not risen to such heights of wealth without appropriate theatre and could well see reason for humility.

We pleaded but every time she sat before the smug face of the Eletu, she tore into the conspirator, traitor, that man of far more unprintable names, whose shadow had brought the darkest times into Lagos.

Her slender form would lean forward, her face a hideous mask of ultimate disgust and rage, her breasts would heave as she attacked each council-members. It was beautiful and unwise.

On the last day, the council fined Kosoko heavily, assumed my innocence and granted Opolu death by hanging for witchcraft.

There was a collective shudder. The council could exile a royal, flatten his pocket, fine her business and it had done all this in the five centuries of Lagos.

It did not order executions. In the silence, the Eletu Ika announced the impossibility of appeal. The execution was slated following dawn.

She looked at Kosoko, turned to me, beautiful and stern -the way she wanted remembrance -and there was a smile somewhere, I tell you.

Opolu in white cotton glaring against her black body standing on a platform with a rope overhead giving the same triumphant look. Opolu. *Ifemi.*

The people gathered wore uncertain faces. *Was this not going too far?* This was the daughter of a man whose ascent into the pantheon they had just celebrated. Would he not exact vengeance? She looked happy. No, there was something wrong in all this.

But she died and the heavens did not fall. Just in case Osinlokun was playing the long con, the people clamoured for the ogalade to make great offerings to all the Gods -let him find no allies but plentiful food and forget the call of war.

Opolu died and there was no state funeral. Her body was to be tossed into the evil forest East of Ikirun but the Eletu proposed a public dump into the sea. She who gave homes would have none.

It was an expression of parlimaentary power to natives and Europeans alike. There was one equal to viscount lamb in Lagos.

For extra measure the Eletu had slaves dig up her revered mother, dragged the corpse before the council, a whore from Egbaland, and dumped the dead and its daughter. The third of September that 1839.

Heaven did not fall but as the peasants believed it might they were given the week off for easy response to emergencies. They gathered at the shrines first and afterwards in the capital square.

This loose congregation posed no danger to the council but now members of the Ogboni began to question if there was any difference between Court and Parliament.

Opolu may have been singled out as royalty but she was a wealthy trader too. There was the twenty-acre farmland north of the lagoon, the almost two thousand slaves and the profits of their petty trade and three baracoons holding another two thousand bodies for sale.

She owned shares in the SS Peterson and SS Bights. Her house in Oniru was built of bricks and the people said she ate on silver plates like the Queen of England. Was private property now in question?

She had the largest single holding of slaves, 3,800. Almost one thousand of those served her in partnerships -petty shops, as captains of canoes paying a stipend for each trip, as small-Time slave traders themselves.

Of the five hundred resident on her vast estate, she was rumoured to have slept with all the males and a select few of the females. The rest worked on her farms, sustaining themselves and the Princess on produce and sale. She made €5000 every solstice and had acquired suitable insolence.

The council executed her. Aware popular will was swinging against their sail, the Akarigbere invited the *Ifa* to give testimony that Opolu was a witch. It ended its investigations of King and court. It affirmed the twenty percent tax.

Still Opolu tormented the Eletu. Her belongings were confiscated by the palace adding to its strength and revenue. Her death was the rallying cry of the conservatives. For Kosoko and I, there was remembrance. I cannot say more, I tell you.

The Europeans spoke of market stability and Porto Novo. The Badagry army disbanded without a word to their old bene-factor, leaving the priests free for propanganda as far as Ilorin.

The Eletu Odibo was suddenly the cunning tortoise awaiting comeuppance in moonlight stories from Ouidah to Benin. When he fell ill under the cares of office, the world was convinced Osin-lokun had acquired the friendship of, at the least, Esu.

Convinced there was no better moment to strike, Kosoko announced war. The disgrace of his mother and death of his two siblings undoubtedly smarted. But Kosoko announced war be-cause Oluwole had thrown in his lot with Odibo. Mischief was certain to come again.

Oluwole was the first son of Oba Adele. As he was convinced the Osinlokuns actively sought to rid him of his inheritance, he had spurred the investigations. He said rubbish more than half the time. Oshodi slept with men or Kosoko slept with his father's wives or Opolu slept in the blood of slave babies.

But he mentioned the Igbakaun too and publicity never served intelligence agencies. We had the swede, the armies which remebered Osinlokun, the lower chiefs resentful of Akari-gbere influence and palace slaves. Kosoko would not depend upon the perpetually late guilt of a mob.

Adele did not give him approval, as the prince would claim in every late-night rendezvous with chiefs sympathetic to his cause.

The Oba, who had loved His niece like his daughter, was docile now. He had won the major battles of his life, crown and royal taxes, and there need be no more deaths in his house.

But he did not clearly dissuade the prince. There were hints of preference over Oluwole and support in a civil war. When Kosoko struck, Adele refused to pronounce war; instead he ban-ished the prince, placed bounties on his supporters and confiscated their properties.

And so although it is called the Cocoayam Civil War, Ogun Ewe Koko, by the public, it was nothing beyond a disorganized protest. It was loud and vehement like the storm of Osinlokun's death. Vanished that quick. A few men died for a metre and the rest went home.

The government and its expatriate traders referred to it- before, during and after -as "an incisive police action".

They have a point. It lasted three days.

WE THE PEOPLE

No man born of woman owns himself as much as he would. But Adedibu owned nothing. He was born as the fourteenth son of a chieftain in Tivland, certain to acquire nothing from family.

Sent to live with his uncle, a blacksmith in Erobo, his wages were withheld until the end of his apprenticeship and repayment of the cloths, food and housing his master provided.

One idle afternoon, while he considered this matter of natural poverty under the Iroko tree next to the smithy, a band of Egba slave-raiders took him captive.

There was no trade. Certain bands found it more sinecure to be retained by a wealthy trader rather than face shifting market demand and seasons without bodies.

They stripped him of the clothes he hadn't paid for and, putting him into chains, shipped him alongside a hundred and twenty captives in a deep canoe down the lagoon.

They put him into a baracoon where he did not own the shit reaching up his ankles, the food four hundred men scrambled upon or the thoughts of bitterness which was in all of them and yet not.

His days were spent in two-feet of a baracoon and he had no idea when it changed hands from Opolu to the Palace.

Oba Adele ordered a rapid auction of the slaves in the baracoons and military training of the domestic slaves. A week after the police action, two hundred royal respresentatives presented 4,700 men and women at the docks.

Messengers on foot, winged, fetish or in boats sped towards Ouidah, Calabar and down the Volta to inform partners of a slave glut.

Conservatives praised the King for his tough reforms and the resultant economic revival. Liberals sang of Eletu.

The result was London's despatch of ten more steamboats in the Royal Navy's Anti-Slavery Squadron. In Westminster papers,the port of Lagos was henceforth called alongside Dahomey's - the great twin bastions of Slavery.

Over-supplied and heavily regulated, prices should have fallen. But inspite of the heavy risk, perhaps because of this, slave prices and their demand shot up.

European traders considered the prices they would fetch after the starvation of the Middle Passage if they could gather bodies at present rates.

The natives considered that with more traders pouring into the town and the Squadron already stretched thin, prices would rise alongside an European frenzy as the first ships reached America.

Against everybody's desire, the prices rose overnight. The largest inventory, that of the palace, brought in eighteen thousand pounds. Four hundred Orisas were the idea of infinity. They knew a shilling. *Eighteen thousands pounds of those?* It was a giddy feeling.

Families mortgaged their lands, sold their cows and apprenticed their children for immediate cash. Families made down payments -a leg this time and ear another -or banded together to buy one man.

Before Opolu, a body was thirteen pounds in the native market. In the immediate months after her death, it rose to two hundred pounds. One could buy and resell the next day to Europeans on a coast six miles away for six hundred. The wise hoarded.

Adedibu was one such body. From the palace, he was purchased for thirty-nine by the Ariyo Family who soon doubted the entire enterprise, and resold each slave for one-seventy.

The second buyer of Adedibu was the palace caught in the hysteria it had created. An anonymous trader bought him off palace hands at two-fifty.

With the baracoons full and makeshift warehouses raising rents, it made sense that he was placed in a canoe and sent back across the lagoon.

But in Tivland, they were set free, given weapons and taught to fight. The palace had bought him again.

There was lax security. There was talk of killing the scanty officers and parting in so many different ways as to ensure some reached home. The guards hinted anyone could walk without bloodshed. But now something came across Adedibu.

This generally unfortunate being,addressed the men as follows:

"Ti won ba so fun o pe ki o lo si ile, se o mo ile re? Tani yoo ki yin nile? Who will greet you at home? Je ki a bura fun ara wa ki a di idile kan. Je ki a ni owo. Lehinna je ki a sin arakunrin Opolu ki a gbesan iku re"

This was treason. The guards joined the cheer. The slaves elected him commander.

They marched upon Lagos. Their apperance triggered a mass protest. Kosoko himself appeared before them at Iga Idunganran -if before they would follow their commander for gold, they would follow Kosoko for pride.

Ah, he fired their souls, that handsome prince. He spoke in his "I am", in the same sort of way Moses must have sounded. The crowd sang "Kabiyesi o"

In three days they would be chased out of Lagos, fully mercenary, their motto: owo ati kosoko. Money and Kosoko. They stretched north into ilorin, west into Whydah and east into Benin. They wore red danshikis with cowries on the underside crafted in specific order, gave passwords, spent the day in vigorous training and the night in sober sleep.

This was the beginning of the Olushoba regiment which saved Kosovo's life two times before he was king and nine times afterwards, won Lagos two times and lost it three, transformed into the *Igbimo Ominira,* Freedom Council, as loosely-affiliated Robin Hoods through-out Yoruba Land only to reform itself under an aged Adedibu, less one Hand but freeman now, as Consular Guard and Lagos Constabulary for the British.

EXILES

A little girl-child in a sailor's yard is obvious. The sea might be at tide and a man's body at full mast when the girl passes by in floating sun-dress. The sun blinds him to the age. He will cat-call.

Then there are the little boys, alternately beggars and thieves, who will harry her on her journey through. One of their number is always the gallant little man quieting the others and bobbing up at her side with the air of an English gentlemen to say

"Say, Miss, Can I help you with sum'n"

And she would laugh and cry as her mood gives and perhaps tell the gallant lad, to the amusement of the oarsmen where she lived.

The girl who walked through did not have time for such nonsense. In her satchel, she carried a letter of the utmost importance and if she liked one of the boys, what did it matter when she and her mistress, as yet, had nowhere to stay?

Kosoko had left the ship the same october night it docked at Porto Novo. He did not say goodbye, merely left letters in his room dealing with domestic matters.

One was addressed to his wife, another to Tapa, and a third in the satchel was for a certain Joachim Marino who lived in the finer section of the city, the Roque De Marnes. For me there was nothing. There was no forwarding address.

The harbor of that great city was the angle of an L. One could walk forward and meet the warehouses now stocked with dry fish and pepper and palm oil but still reeking of the host of black bodies it was originally built for. There were alleys of beer parlours and gambling stations.

The warehouses were next to the tenements where the sailors and craftsmen lived, a bitter slum rife with prostitution and murder. It gave way to the second market and led, through a lonely stretch familiar bandits, into the farmlands and community of the Sa Doe. Hobessian land.

The left gate of the harbour was the city proper with the King's palace, two churches, the ply-wood factories, the palm-oil presses and the fortress of Ipsa.

A respectable stretch with block-houses and family offices lay in between these. There were paved mud-paths going off this stretch into barracks and the fancy town-houses used by the Bishop and Gezo's administrator.

It was busy in daylight and quiet at night. A fine suburb whose most sordid sight was the homeless shelter organised by the catholic church. But even this was merely the business district and considered with disdain by those noveau rich resident in the Roque De Marnes.

The Roque began with the portuguese fort now assigned to the English and housed an impoverished ambassador. Past the fort lay the white houses of the Porto Novan elite, the bankers and heavy traders.

Our little girl reached the Roque and daintily climbed its steps to be stopped by the guard who told her to scurry off.

Removing all gaiety, she raised her small five foot frame into royal bearing "My name"she said "is Matilda, daughter of King Alo of the Ijapa, captive in Ijesa War, lady in waiting upon Arabesola, rightful Queen of Lagos and Badagry. My mistress sends me with this letter to Senor Jose"

The guard cast her look down her body but he had not yet spoken fetid when she noticed his tribal marks and swore in Egba dialect whereupon the startled man opened the gates and let her through.

The winding boulevard brought her to the corsican, a sad small cafe. The men and women who frequented it stayed drunk all of the time.

Work was considered distateful in the Roque, to be avoided if possible, and the afternoons were spent in dalliances, playing cards, and drinking wine.

Every hour or so, the french patron's voice rang out over the room in search of a regular whose business associate or servant or wife had come seeking but even that was no interruption to the laughter and brawls.

It rang out that moment. "Jose! Jose! *Uma Jovem* here to see you"

"I have always told you if it is my daughter, she is a minha filha"

The patron laughed. His portuguese was exhuasted "*Assez avec ton argot iberique.* She is not your daughter"

He came, brash and red-faced, his petticoat an open frame for the belly. "What can I do for you, *pequena senhora*"

"Kosoko" she said simply as she handed the letter to him.

He grunted in approval and tore it open. It was hilarious, she would tell me, how his nonchalance transformed into incredulity -his eyes widened, his disbeliving grunts grew more forceful and when he was done, he shouted "este nao e o fim de tudo"

"Where are they?"

"At the port."

He grabbed the collars of a young man sitting by the door, "run,get my coach"

It would be her firm conviction that he was a good man. I agree that he often went beyond duty but I had traded with Jose Miguel.

I knew the hefty concessions, venetian pounds of flesh, he would lose without an Osinlokun on the throne. He was too close to the palace not to be cut off and it was in his interest to provide shelter, pray for better times, buy gratitude. He was a good businessman.

THE RAMPARTS
OF LAGOS

I n Lagos, Arabesola had had a lively and sharply cut face. Her eyes, brown and forceful, were as gay as a young girl's and she was kind, cheerful, a practical joker so mild one never took offense.

This was the girl, woman now, whose fancy for Kosoko broke her bethrotal with the Eletu Odibo, transformed the politics of Lagos for the next 26 years, invited the British, and inaugurated colonialism. An ebony face launching a thousand ships. Black Helen.

Kosoko often slept early and so we would go, all of us, to attend upon the princess and her ladies and her witty conversation was light, none of the depth to which her husband's mind often plunged and which grew tasking for the most patient outsider.

In Porto Novo, there was no court and the pregnancy made her round; the fences were the first extent of that spirit.

She refused. Soon her interest in trade became a Roque scandal. Her long walks down the piazza where her slave girls sold everything from brocade to beads was accompanied with applause or headshakes -sign of enterprise or evidence of non-royal blood.

She had commandeered Jose's garden, turned it into an adventure for the lecher's three prim daughters, and sufficient food for the household.

Then she argued with Jose on his prodigality until the portuguese turned over his finances and the textile concern to her.

Arabesola was a yoruba woman, a term Osinlokun once called synonymous with 'peppery mouth'. When the nurse insisted on moving her to the hospital for regular assistance, she had the nurse placed on leave by the hospital and on her domestic payroll by Joachim and kept the lady in the vast room "for comfort and baby"

Shortly after the nurse took up residence, Arabesola bought thirteen yoruba women off the ships and lodged them in the rooms opposite or besides hers.

As she explained to an exasperated Joachim, a baby born without the presence of many women would be socially deficient all through life and so the voices rang out all hours -in quarrelsome loudness or sober gossip in her quarters, punctuated with the laughter conducive to good fortune.

So long as his wealth and leisure grew, and it did, the Portuguese did not mind. He purchased a house close to the Corsican for his independence, bought a new steamboat -the very one which would return Kosoko to Lagos, -and a two-horse carriage.

Arabesola moved to the upper floor of Sacramento and peopled it with the daughters and ladies in waiting.

She wrote often to me, dictating the gossip of Porto Novo and asking of her husband through Matilda's hands.

She worried about the weather, so unlike Lagos, and sent me letters to be posted from my station to her relatives. Once, she asked if I had ever met this strange animal called the *Esube* and requested that its meat be dried and sent to her.

I assured her the mythical creature, a native leviathan, had been captured and was being prepared for shipping since it was so large that three ships had to be nailed together for its voyage.

She said she laughed upon receipt of my absurdity and I thank God because between her depressive moods of pregnancy and the circumstances of Porto Novo which glittering though it was was neither palace nor home, Arabesola felt lonely.

Now she stood at the head of the flight of stairs and for the first time I saw vulnerability on her beautiful face. She said "The baby is coming. Find my husband, Dada"

"Should I call the doctor?"

Matilda snickered. "*O je Okunrin. O wa dara*"

"But you look so pale, your Highness"

Sola smiled then, as though she too were afraid.

"Dada I want to see my husband. I want to know if he is alive or dead. Mo fe lati mo boya omo mi yoo rii Eko".

Her words had grown high-pitched and breathless, her hands had gripped the banidster, and her form had hunched ever so slightly over the belly but still she stood with firm eyes and that piteous smile.

I bowed. I heard the scream at the bottom of the stairs.

There were servants downstairs moving about with grave faces. It might have been the rememberance of Kosoko whose absence had almost certainly resolved into death in household gossip.

Or merely that regal solemnity which attends the mystery of birth or death. The house was quiet, punctuated only by Arabesola in her sharp gasps and her involuntary screams like the pitiful whelp of a dog kicked in the belly.

I met Jose at the door, the doctor in tow. They promptly set about disturbing the fine equilibrium of eventful silence.

The loud voice of the Master asked "Where is she?" and the doctor, a man fully buttoned up in the self-important gravity of his profession and sweating as a result, set his bag on the mahogany centre-table and asked in equally loud voice "Might two servants be assigned here?"

In such a moment, where the soul becomes profoundly religious and earthly Masters may be safely dispensed with, the servants ignored the two white men.

I told Jose wryly that he ought to stay out of it. Madame go vex. He fell into a whisper as he pointed to the princess' room and said "There?"

I nodded.

"Is she okay"Another nod.

"I brought the doctor" and this time it sounded like an apology.

"You can take him in" I chuckled "Allow me reach the corsican first." The doctor pulled a seat next to the requisitioned table and sat in a huff.

"And what about my daughters, minha amiga?"

A servant mentioned they had left to the Piazza that morning for the fitting of some gowns. "Then we should await the celebration at the Corsican then" and off we went, doctor in tow.

Into these circumstances, Prince Tade was born. It makes no difference to a child but to be born in exile is a half-truth, like rain halfway through harmattan and courier of all its heat.

The yorubas in Porto Novo trooped to the Roque -there were defiant talking drums upsetting the portuguese tranquility and the many-coloured adire brought gifts and songs and advice.

Jose outdid himself for this heir of Kosoko, declaring free drinks at the cafe three days in a row, having the fort fire a twenty-one gun salute on the day of the naming ceremony and gifting the little boy a turkish sword which he swore the sultan had given his great-grandfather.

Matilda's letter had come ten days before this happy event and I had decided upon travel. It is a stupid thing for a full-grown man, a man disillusioned by the fetid fate of love in life and haunted by the memories of Opolu but I had never pretended wisdom.

In those months of letters where the words had often been Arabe's, I had fallen in love with the delicate tilt of Matilda's hands. It occured to me, and seemed eminently sensible at the time, that one could not write so beautiful unless harmony marked her face and soul.

I was in Lagos in the barely visible role of tax inspector. Idafe, Ibukun and Idaro had returned to the palace as slaves. There were Kosoko's siblings and Opolu's employees. We were everywhere but only barely effective.

The Oba Oluwole had died in a gunpowder explosion and people said it was the work of the Gods. Akitoye, surviving uncle of Kosoko had taken the throne with hesitation. He made a point of asking after the Prince often.

I handled Arabesola's correspondence, met the Olusoba wherever it was, reached the swede about once each month, brought word from our friends and of our enemies. Idafe, Ibukun and Idaro sent me whispers.

There was the untouchable Ayomikun in Badagry and, with her husband and sons still on the run, her house was a way-station for those putting as much distance as they could to the vindictive arms of the Eletu.

Our sympathisers among the chiefs and the traders were

quiet but their letters to Kosoko, which I always faithfully delivered to Arabe, pledged service. The Swede was a decent citizen with allies in the households of all Akarigbere.

But matilda's letter reached Lagos and informed me the baby was due. I had set sail. Arrived. Loved. And here was my *amour courtois,* that ancient curse of knights and demi-gods; recovering the Prince.

I waited in the corsican long enough to hear mother and baby were safe, good news for him, then I thanked Jose for his hospitability, sent letters to the Olusoba to meet me at Whydah, sent my dagger for a keepsake to Matilda and climbed aboard the SS *Diligente* to set sail at dusk.

AN INITIATE

Oshodi Tapa, Adedibu and I had always known exactly where he was. But it is a rare kindness to stand at distance when a man does not wish to be found, to not gaze upon the unconscious naked. We gave it.

At the edge of a universe he once lorded, Kosoko walked the shore, kept his house and counsel, and became Man.

There were no foolish faces of praise, no attendants trailing him with umbrellas large enough to hide from God and self, and no Lethe between the thighs of a black woman.

These comforts had been ripped from his hands and there was only a glancing pain before the joy of liberty confronted him. He walked the shore and picked pieces of himself.

One night, he stood on a boulder naked watching the waves break. In another, he danced the *bata* until he collapsed into the white sand to wake up with thunder and tide.

He would sit at the market, tobacco pipe in hand, and watch the day's toil end. He paid indecent attention when the dogs mated at his feet.

It did not take long for the villagers to call him mad, though they knew only half the extent of his proclivities. Society does not like the unusual, the indifferent, the sure.

It did not take long for the Gods to come to him as gift of

solitude and talent of the mad. He would sit at the door to his hut in prayer and a chicken would walk inside.

Fish greeted him at the shore, and if he sat at a stall, fortune would make it her abode through the day.

It did not take long for the villagers to call him an Orisa. They brought gifts and sick children, daughters and inquiries, sacrifices and a sly complaint against a neighbour.

Kosoko quickly learnt his protests had no effect and so he sat with his back against a wall and listened. Sometimes he would fall asleep in this way and wake up to find his visitor looking askance.

He would give any nonsensical phrase on the tip of his tongue and watch the awed look of the devotee.

Prophecy does not work like a well. One must spit with confidence and watch the river form. Kosoko was good at it. He disdained wealth and grew richer.

His new reputation served his solitude well. A red thread on the ground before the hut would hold a queue for days.

In the market, they gave him the highest honours and the largest berth. And when he stood at the shore, the boats came in early lest the Gods were kept waiting. Divinity demands propitiation.

We had known where he was. I decided he would need a guard of honour. He would enter Porto Novo and then Lagos flanked by men willing to die for him. If Akitoye wanted him back, here was no suppliant but a royal.

But I should have warned the Olushoba. War does not live everywhere, with dead bodies and the buzzing quiet except of flies or a startled congregation of vultures.

Indoors and in its corners, war is hunger and sickness and breaches in the wall; it is inside bodies too, in insomnia and resignation.

But on the other side, the market was open and alive, and the conflict of Lagos was something happening far away.

It had no concern for the prostitutes suggesting a better use of money before the saddled soldiers reached the first of thatched stalls of Whylah.

It held no concern for foul-mouthed traders putting up chickens and waving 'adire' as they jostled beside the fatigued horses.

No concern, at the moment, for the forty-nine Olushoba who had ridden night and day and a half, to enter Owunde market, thirsty with shaven heads glistening in the unrelenting noon.

So when Adedibu ordered the whip for trader and prostitute, the response was anger and not the craven fear of a beaten people.

They tossed tomato water at the armed men, threw catfish which was promptly stolen in the pressing crowd, and cursed the ancestry of the riders in thirteen Yoruba dialects and in Nupe, Bagani, and Eremo languages.

It was a good thing a Marshal was passing through the same moment and purely fortunate that his shrill cry of "In the name of the Chacha" could be heard above the din; because war changes residence often.

More marshals rode up to the market disturbance, surrounded the party to collect horse and weapon from each man, and escorted the party into the palace courtyard, one edge of which held six or seven pits –vast water vats each twelve-foot deep and eight-foot long for the comfort of government and royalty now repurposed into prisons, their carved wooden covers pierced in a dozen places for air.

Fired clay had kept the vat cold through the African heat, and now it held the varied stench of urine and faeces at different stages of rot. Their pit was empty but its past inhabitants had left memorials and, after descending by a quickly withdrawn ladder, the group was forced to gather in two groups at a clean corner and a stretch of virgin clay along the east wall.

Their horses were being taken care of, the first marshal said, and "all of this would be sorted out soon, I am sure. The Chacha would request your presence at the palace as soon as he wakes up"

It was always Folorunsho who spoke, always with venom enough for forty-eight men.

"By Sango, you will suffer for this, you miserable bastards. You do not know what you have done. By Sango, I will set this village on fire before nightfall. And who is this useless chacha who sleeps at noon"

He turned to his colleagues "You know what they are doing, don't you? They are dividing our horses among their besieged calabash heads. They won't even tell their Chacha whatever. Hey you" he said to the Marshal in pidgin Egba dialect "You're watering the horses? Water. Awa san ju esin lo. Give us water" and he made a jugging motion.

The marshal promised them Water but he didn't want any shouting. His plea only agitated Folorunsho whose saliva could not fly twelve-foot.

"I will shout. I will shout. You vagabonds won't tell him he has new prisoners, would you? By Sango, these bureaucrats are criminals everywhere. I'll shout so loud his royalty will stumble from sleep asking for your head. But what sort of lazy monarchs live in these parts? Sleeping in the afternoon like feeble Europeans"

"He is European" The moment the last plank was firmly in

place and the marshal gone, laughter began.

It began from the barrel-chested dark-skinned commander from his corner of urine-smelling clay and spread through every man until Folorunsho tittered despite himself.

"Well, *aja-binu*, you have landed us in another trouble" Adedibu said. *Aja Binu*, dog-rage, was his pet name for the rash lieutenant and personal guard.

"Forgive me Oga, but this bunch of shit-smelling stupid villagers need lessons and, by Sango, I am too willing to provide it. They dare treat warriors this way; a hundred vile curses and every disease of Agagan follow their descendants" Folorunsho said.

He was still gingerly walking the sides of the pit, around patches of darkness and foul shit, searching for a hold in the smooth hard clay. "And an European chief? *Olorun ko*"

"Come, cease your search. We should all rest, eh? We had no money for food anyway" the commander said. "Come. Ibitaiye, what do you know about this people? Tell me again"

Ibitaiye was another lieutenant, and he sat cross-legged in the other oasis, eyes at half-mast, when the commander's voice reached him and jolted him awake.

"Whydah used to be richer than Lagos. It still makes money. If there is an european chief, it must be Francisco De Souza. I thought such things were moonlight stories. So the Minons are real?"

"The women soldiers? Impossible" kayode said.

"I had said so about a white chief"

"Hmm"

It was obvious he knew nothing more so Adedibu reminded the men to rest. And they did, leaning against the wall or another body, head bent forward with chin on chest, as they drifted into sleep.

By the time the Olushoba was up and pacing the pit again, the sun had slanted –almost three hours by the distance the sun-spots had travelled along the clay. The familiar marshal raised the plank soon after that ballet round the edges of the pit.

"The Chacha has heard of the market matter. He doesn't want mercenaries to feel unwelcome in his town but you under-stand we have rules. People are tense here" and he knocked his forefinger against his head as another plank was raised and the ladder returned.

"If you will follow me, I will show you your quarters. Tomor-row is a very big day. The Priest Kosoko is giving the Chacha a farewell blessing. Everybody is busy"

"Kosoko?" Adedibu asked

"Yes. The Great Priest"

"Priest?"The laughter spread again.

"You thieves. What about our horses, our bags? Or your re-port to the viceroy has us on foot?" Folorunsho said

The Marshall spoke without the slightest hint of irony. "As criminals, military service is a privilege. If you like, you can stay here but I would suggest you join the army and get some air. Your belongings would be returned after your service. Or when next your case comes up before the Chacha. These things take some time"

Adedibu spoke "Tell your Chacha that we are servants of royalty. Our master would not be glad we have been treated this way."

Distinct worry replaced nonchalance on the official's face. Royal servants carried diplomatic privileges and to offend them could well bring warfare in wild times. "Who is your master"

"Oba Kosoko"

"Kosoko"

"Yes. King of Lagos"

He shook his head in confusion "I will tell him. Wait here"

It took an hour before he came back, three servants of the Chacha marching behind him with forty-nine folds of kaftan between them.

His smile was different, appeasing as he helped each man out of the pit and offered his "personal apologies, and those of my sovereign" forty-nine times.

He made jokes to the mercenaries as he led them down one hallway and up another of the Palace, but they remained sullen in the embroidered kaftan. There was a look of relief on his pudgy black face as he pointed them into the throne room and walked away with the servants.

The throne room was made of fired clay with intricate drawings, fire stands and animal skulls on three walls.

The throne, carved mahogany with history drawn on its nine-foot backrest and gold-plated arm-rests, rested against the fourth, a large rug of sewn leopard skin spread before it to half the room. The Chacha was quite intentional with his africanity.

There were a servant on one side of the throne, and a curtained door set into the wall on the other side.

On the long sides, there were two other doors opposite each other and two guards stood beside each. The guard held long-spears, the ikue imported from the fulanis, and crescent swords hung from a belt around their short wrapper.

They stood immobile, like black marble statues from Nok, the hint of a roving eye in impassive faces. The Olushoba stood just before the throne-side door, facing the ChaCha who was in heated conversation, gesticulating with his tall wiry frame almost reaching the eaves every-time he nodded vigorously.

Franscisco De Souza was portuguese-brazilian. He had helped Gezo ascend the throne of Dahomey through a coup d'etat. He traded in palm oil and gold. His trading company had sold half a million slaves. He was possibly the richest man south of the equator. They could wait.

Finally Souza dismissed the fellow. Oshodi Tapa and I were brought in. We mingled with the Olushoba -they considered us honorary members -as we waited again for the Chacha. He smiled broadly at us and clapped his hands.

With a vanguard, Kosoko entered by the eastern door. He was a new man. There was something unreal about him. You felt it self-evident that this man was a god. The entire cohort shouted "Kabiyesi"

A VERY CIVIL WAR

Oshodi Tapa who had sat fidgeting by the door now cried out "The needful thing is to fight, to fight and kill them. Give me the army of Badagry and I will end this in one week. We talk and talk and do nothing".

I replied that the rash are really only cowards of thought and Tapa, a magnificent fighter, responded warmly. We wrangled while Kosoko, positively delighted, gave an encouraging *hmm* or *haa* to this person or that

Kosoko was at peace that evening, in a way I had not seen since the wedding night. He had the faint hint of a smile, a look which reminded me of a Babalawo's face at the summons of a spirit -optimistic caution, that is what it was, gazing through the mist to see who was coming but almost certain it was a friend by the tilt

He had always had a royal dignity about him. His brief training at the courts of Benin had refined him, granted the diplomatic mastery and the sophistication Lagos did not have. In Bahai, he had become familiar with the Europeans and the barely cloaked mission of imperialism.

His military service as a recruit in the Bini Army on the Sapele River and a lagos commander against the Egba had given him working knowledge of tactics. He was a careful judge of men.

A prophet too. The personal charisma, the fervent self-belief, the hint of friality had made him an idol among us.

The troops called him "proud bastard" to his face but they willingly would bleed. In the nights, when he was away from the lanterns or asleep or even in the brief instant of a shadow, his skin glistened. The halo of Orunmila.

He had returned to Lagos quite prepared for peace. We recieved gifts and he was titled the Oloja of Ereko. The Eletu had gone on voluntary exile and the Oba sought to recall him. When the Prince remonstrated, Akitoye called him an upstart who could not define his administration.

There would be war. That much was certain. Town-criers had gone about in a war of words for a fortnight. The palace had announced a conscription and found an exodus. Nobody wanted to fight this Kosoko.

He stopped us and said at lenght that he would fight and a shout passed through the two dozen men sitted around the fire. "But it will not be like the cocoyam war".

This meant two things: the first, immediately grasped by all the ambitious of which I was chief, that Kosoko held command. He was a brilliant strategist and wanted no disorder.

The second, less arcane, implication was that the coming war would not be a mass offensive with the palace for target. The cocoayam war had been ludo; men had been thrown haphazardly against Iga Idunganran and Eletu.

The Oba's impregnable defenses allowed them patience until sanctions began to hurt and bounties were public. A small force had pushed out the recalcitrant on the third day.

This time, Kosoko explained, we would take the countryside, the farms and villages, successively winning over to our cause by pernury or example more chieftains of the landed aristocracy.

"It will be a determined but civil war" He told us.

To defend each of these landownings would task the four-thousand-strong garrison in Lagos. Adeniyi said they would require ten thousand mercanaries to hold the vital points alone, an impossible number for a crown stripped of its rent and food.

"Let him be King in the palace while we hold the villages. *Won yoo so o ni okuta*"

Oshodi, who believed the cocoayam war failed because of execution and not poor strategy, foregone conclusion since he was the prime architect, refused to budge.

"Let him be King in the palace? Do you think he will starve when the British are his friends? And what of Benin who, invited, will open a second front against us? We will then be the ones to starve because the villagers will turn on us, returning to those former masters who though no better, are at-least familiar".

Several crazy schemes were suggested as a remedy to this problem. Shooting all the royal birds, falcons, headed to Benin.

Kidnapping british traders in badagry to negotiate a blockade on the capital. Even attacking Benin first before settling in for the strategy of occupation.

Again it was Kosoko who showed that superiority of intellect which is the true divine right to rule. "We should gather a navy".

This sounded like the craziest idea of all and many believed he said it in jest. Ayo mentioned Opolu's former employees, most of them still ran the boats on behalf of the palace. Akinmosa said we might as well send a written declaration of war -an European imprudence,

Ibukun reminded the laughing men that he was the descendant of Aje, first son of Olokun, the God of the Ocean, to which some wag responded that Thomas Hamilton, First Lord of the Admiralty, of whom slavers had heard much, must be his third cousin.

Kosoko shared in this merriment a time then said "I am serious"at which the room went deathly still.

The average yoruba man could swim and sail, yes, but he saw the sea for commerce and the land for farming. In military terms, the sea was for transportation and the land for fighting.

"The boats are not the problem. Opolu still has three hundred canoes and four flagships, vessels which escaped the Eletu Odibo and the palace. They are at Epe" I did not mention I had been running them as a private enterprise to fund individual expenses and the resistance.

"We can mount six cannons on each and build a small cover like the ones used in the delta by small trading houses. But who would sail in them" Nobody raised hands.

Odunsi asked "Do they have to sail?"I laughed. "See, we cannot be like the British immediately. We can hold a blockade at the sea. It is our ports, after all, and so long as our two navies are peaceably, we should have no contest"

"No, the contest will come" Kosoko said. "The English Navy is not here merely to stop the slave trade. They are here to own the markets and sell us their goods, whether we need them or not, and to do that they will first take the ports then take the government. Opolu's ships are fine for this war but we must rapidly build our own ships at Sapele because after Akitoye we must fight the British Consul. We need sailors"

There were many of us who scoffed inwardly at this because the British appeared quite ready to leave us alone if we left the slave trade unlike the portuguese and french.

It would take many years to understand their civility as

merely the polish upon fine boots accustomed to kicking doors and idi.

"This war would be different." He pointed at each man as he spoke. "The land army would hold the ground and our new navy will attack Lagos. It is not a war of waiting, Oshodi." But it was.

"Opolu's boats, under you Olamide, would threaten the Bini at Sapele and along the coastline. You will not engage unless the Oba sends an army against our positions in Eko."

"Another two hundred commandeered from traders and outfitted at Badagry would be led down the lagoon by Ariyo, there to bombard the city and ignore the British. The army of Badagry will be divided into three, under *arakunrin mi* Odunsi, Akinmosa and Adeniyi"

"To ensure speedy communications with the army, we must take and hold Idanre" Oshodi ventured. He wanted command.

"Yes. And I have just the man to do it. You, Tapa, and your men will be with me. We need a station on the lagoon to deter British landings. If nothing happens, we will land in Eko "

As there was no talk of assignments for myself or Adedekun or the half-dozen other senior officers, I assumed we will be shared as deputies.

Kosoko announced he would move with a large retinue to camp with the various land divisions, confusing the Igbakaun spies since we were unsure of their loyalty.

The asogbon would be in the dark. "In three weeks, the King would seek to flee Lagos. We will allow him safe passage here"

At this last bit, a murmur of dissent rose. "You are being soft on him because he brought you back from an unjust exile"

"No I am being soft on him because we will need a face for the British. Akitoye is hated by the people and loved by the British. So long as he is their option, we have nothing to fear. It will be easy to let the Oba of Benin see his man cavourting with the same white-men encroaching on his empire and ally with me, rightful king of Lagos and true defender of Benin"

"What about the Eletu?" Gbenga asked.

One had to be familiar with the face to see the brief glint of granite, the momentary hardening of its amiable features, at the mention of Odibo. Kosoko looked meaningfully at me and said "Let us focus on Lagos".

I understood my task clearly and the next night, I and the full Olusoba regiment, four hundred men, set out for Ajara to which the Eletu had fled. Adedekun went east to recruit sailors at calabar.

The Olusoba were grossly outnumbered but more men could not be spared without public notice of the vendetta in an army where the Eletu was still held in high esteem.

Ajara was a small settlement, about a thousand women and children, built around a palm plantation east of Badagry.

It afforded Odibo considerable revenue and, once he had built up a two forts staffed with twelve hundred trained slaves, adequate protection.

The northern road from Badagry ran through one of these forts and its flanks were protected by the friendly towns of tado and iseki whose chiefs could each muster men our number and better equipped.

I took them therefore down the coast, ostensibly as a vanguard for the division under Tapa; but at the bridgehead, which we reached at dusk, we turned into Itiade and rode for four hours with the excuse of an alarm that the chieftain sought to harass our crossing.

There we camped thirteen days while the commanders moved their men, piecemeal to the opposite shore. The boatsmen ferried Ibukun and Tapa all at fair price only to return from this profitable venture into Ariyo's draft.

Kosoko stayed behind to supervise the armaments then he too crossed, ostentiously, towards Ibukun.

Only then did I inform the regiment of our true objective and they were so overjoyed, these men who lived for blood-feuds and wealth, that they suggested we strike camp immediately and gun for Ajara.

I refused and Adedibu conceded. Things had to be timed with the occupation force to avoid mutiny in the badagry army.

I kept them busy with raids upon Egbaland for another fortnight; then, once the towns had been taken and the two fleets in position, we rode for Ajara from the North.

It was the same evening that had Kosoko facing the aide. Fashanu was the best of the young men, twenty-something years sitting on his wispish face as forty. But he had not yet learnt how to hide fear.

At the moment, gathering up the maps, commandeered from european traders in Gbaji, the aide had a wistful look as though his mind at that moment was editing his own obituary.

There was nothing of the boisterousness of the older men, confident of some god's favour in past conflict, in his small sad face. He did not drink, like most of his age-group who, dissatified with their gourds, sat around the large clay-pots of palmwine and courage.

Noticing Kosoko now faced him, the terror was multiplied at being discovered and a tremor in his hands shook the maps loose so that he rose up into attention, like the British had taught, with the papers rolling towards his superior and his mind unsure whether to bend again or stand straight.

Kosoko picked the papers off the ground and having rolled

them properly, tapped the youth on the shoulder with the bundle. "Why dont you drink?"

Fashanu began to stammer something but Kosoko gave him the maps and asked him to walk through the camp with him. "Tomorrow, you will fight beside me because you are brave. Or are you not?"

There was almost a whimper before the youth said "Sire, I dont think myself brave"

They were outside the tent and right across its entrance were the clay-pots were almost five hundred men polled and passed along gourds with bubling fresh pammy.

Kosoko turned to the left, where the path to the stream cut through the second encampment under his lieutenant, Remi Adebisi.

More than a thousand men camped at the stream believing themselves to be the rear but Remi had bridged the stream and the King walked lazily, with his aide by his side and some servants in tow, as though he was not relocating to his new front.

They had gone some distance into the four kilometre wide bush which seperated both camps before the royal guardsmen rode forward with a white horse for the King.

Kosoko made one dismount and walk behind the slaves to hurry them up while his aide clambered on the french horse and rode beside him.

The procession moved in silence as the sun set and so it confused Fashanu when the King turned to the youth near the outpost and asked "How many men are brave enough to admit it?"

"Admit what, Kabiyesi?"

"Fear."

At that moment, a horn sounded from the watch and the

camp bustled as it readied itself for its King. "I am afraid and it is what convinces me to be strong in the face of this duty. Surely if I had no fear, I would have no conviction and both the effort and its reward would look miserable to me. Do you understand?"

"Yessire"

"Are you brave or are you not?"

"Kabiyesi, I am brave"

"Then you must prove it." and he drew his horse short so that the procession stopped.

"You heard all that was said? And you hold the maps. Tonight you must cross the stream at the other end and reach Idanre road. It is you I choose for that task. When we attack them at Ilosore, they will try to turn around us at Idanre. Tell your men to surrender"

The tremor was back in such violence that the horse became restive under unsure hands. "Sire..."

But Kosoko turned to the commander of his royal guard and asked him to support the youth "with the best guardsmen in yoruba land. No more than fifty"

Then leaving the royal guard and the terrified aide to take a route which cuts off the main path to go along the right bank towards Idanre, Kosoko entered his second camp to happy tumult.

The young aide, whose orbituary now seemed even more relevant for final edits, was the same Fashanu known as *ariran ogun*, or war-seer, and it was his foresight which went beyond Idanre to save Kosoko in the British war.

But at the moment, there was no such strenght because Fashanu's genius had not yet encountered dangerous neccessity.

If his own mind was so reluctant, twenty horsemen and thirty footmen who came up behind his unsteady horse were even more so. But the party obeyed Kosoko and went thirty miles in the thick of the night to hold Idanre by sunrise.

Some god must have warned Akitoye, or perhaps the tumult in the second camp came to his scouts, because the monarch convened his council of war and asked for an offensive on Badagry at first light.

But whether they believed Kosoko remained there with the fearless Ogboni and his guardsmen or because they feared to attack and stake the survival of Eko on a single battle, the generals demurred.

It was impossible, they said, to cross the creek since the goddess was a patroness of the city and would not suffer its enemies to survive its waters.

And if, perchance, they pushed Kosoko there, like a cornered snake he was all the more dangerous. And had he not broken out like that at Ijesa and ransacked the city before the army knew of his escape? It was better to wait.

But Akitoye did not allow it to be settled on that account but asked the agbogbon to move his men back over the lagoon because if Kosoko attacked with his customary boldness, it was best that they faced men who had first battled pitiless nature in going through the swamp.

But here the generals howled. What madness, their polite looks seemed to ask, would allow Kosoko cross and enter Lagos before fighting him.

One general, removing his cap and flogging his breast with it, shouted "We are the cornered snake. Let him come. *Je ki o wa, Kabiyesii, se o ri mi gbon?*"

It would have been wisdom to shake one's body in fright, or atleast one's head in sadness as the powerless Akitoye now did, at such hubris.

Between Ikosi and Ikorodu, forty miles of marshland extended northward from the lagoon. Both armies had kept to the water and it seemed impossible, now they had met themselves, to detach any unit to round the swamp without exposing their centre to a difficult but possible thrust by the enemy across the marshland.

Lagos had two thousand men but it could afford to wait since it was hoping on the british and could leave the town of Ishapa, which ended the swamp, as bait to the Tapa.

The Badagry warriors found it necessary to force the conflict since their numbers were few and they could not hope for victory at Ishapa.

At dawn therefore, seven hundred infantrymen sunk up to their waist marched through the swamp.

To preserve their bodies from leeches and their rifles from the swamp, they wrapped them in cocoyam leaves so that the army appeared a bright olive green penetrating the bog and it is from that strange sight, never before seen in yoruba-land, that the war got its first name.

Having rejected palace couriers asking for an immediate crossing or retreat such that half the attacking army would be at sea, the three generals now ordered the Lagos army into the marsh at Odofin and blundered into a third error.

Perhaps the plan was to force the unprepared badagry army back onto the opposite shore. They would descend and hold an advantage at the edge of the halfway deep. The ranking Asogbon chief, Segun, assured the palace he would eliminate the Badagry threat in one day.

Kosoko had some luck from sibling rivalry. His three armies had merged into one because Akinmosa and Adeniyi who constantly bickered found in Odunsi an arbiter who began to lead.

Segun had ordered his left and right flanks into pincers piercing the ketu and Idanre roads. He would cross the mainforce and watch where Kosoko's men felt obliged to divide and face this new threat. Then driving a wedge between them, they could destroy the army piecemeal.

Now he found that the ridge was one of several small plains where the undulating swamp went down below the knee and after twenty feet it rose up again to the chest.

Mad with the idea of encirclement, Segun would not stop at this error but continued to advance his three positions, their army of artisans finding it hard in the bog.

Segun met Adeniyi's four hundred men first and found no retreat from their concentrated number who pushed against him in every valley while his five hundred men were thrown into confusion.

Each man carried another, two hundred guns above the field and were shooting long before the asogbon caught on.

Men crawled under the swamp to survive. Others ran back uphill, throwing the ranks into disarray and making a disorderly retreat back to Ikorodu.

Segun now abandoned all hopes of encirclement where his weapons and men had suffered from the swamp. He pushed for Badagry.

His two lieutenants, Bamidele and Aruko, were to hold Oja and Odofin and await further instructions.

Segun's brigade ran into Akarakumo and threw the city into great tumult. Requisitions and conscriptions went at a rapid pace.

Odunsi must have had a difficult time persuading Adeniyi to cease pursuit as I did convincing the Olushoba that we needed Segun pushing into Badagry.

Piecemeal, Bamidele was being destroyed by the Akinmosa's division on the outskirts of Lagos. He had been driven back from Odofin into Ifelodun.

Aruko had taken Idanre road, throwing open the sentry and taking Fashanu captive. He found himself surrounded at Oja and surrendered.

Odunsi had landed at Eti-Osa. Kosoko and Oshodi Tapa were off the island, shelling the palace at dawn and dusk, nothing dangerous beyond the impertinence, the mockery of an Oba marooned.

Segun's lines were cut, he was useless so the sole reason for conscription was defensive. He would pledge allegiance to the Eletu Odibo and take the governoship perhaps. The man had fought to save his hide, not to win.

"That is his only use, access to the Eletu. So long as he is unaware that we are here, the Eletu would open his fortress." I fancied I was beginning to earn some respect from the commander.

We heard Eko no longer had security in numbers. Aruko had surrendered, Bamidele was dead. About a thousand men still held the marshland but the Asogbon chiefs were asking for terms of peace.

Three weeks later, a boat crossed the Lagoon into Ifelodun. Akinmosa's men did not see it or any detail of the forty-plus occupants. The company passed through the Idanre road and Fashanu was not on duty. They crossed Oja into Badagry. The throne was empty.

WESTMINSTER

Beecroft was no royal. His hands were, large and rough with bulging veins, were nothing pretty. He was of middle height, with piercing eyes, a flat nose and a chin cut out of granite. He came down to Africa with the awkward gait of the humble.

The opposite, in every way it would seem, of the aristocratic class. Indeed, when placed beside his first chief, Alexander the Governor of Porto Novo, second son to the second son of the Earl of Lancastire, the commissioner cut a poor figure.

But in badagry, head of his own small corner of the British Empire and arbitrator of these three-fifths of human, Beecroft had grown that noble and distinguished air of a man accustomed to command.

The sound of his voice had grown into a sound at once penetrating and melodious, and the former schoolteacher had acquired those manners of high degree which, after strenuous effort, appear unconsciously to mark a man for higher stations.

Armed with etiquette and a worldly knowledge, counterfeit perhaps in coming from books but rivalling that of any peer in England, Beecroft had the rarest coolness -that character stable as a bedrock in both conversation and action that all men would naturally wish him their friend if only for future political favours.

Yet, that afternoon, Kosoko had thrown him on his back. Revealed him for a charlatan. Indeed when Kosoko had asked him of his ancestry, rather than pass off the question as an aristocrat would, with pitying disdain or else a high recitation with the liberty of fiction in a place so far removed from London society, the schoolteacher had grown red about the ears.

Then, fumbling for a plank on which to hold his dignity afloat, he asked the King who an African was to question his Queen's servant.

"Not just any African, mind." Kosoko said in a brilliant affectation of the British accent. "But one who is a royal, like your Majesty. One who owns the land, like your Majesty owns hers. One who is no mere commissioner -indeed has commissioners with more sense of their place in this court or elsewhere, than you appear to do, Sire."

For effect, the King turned on his chair towards me and inquired of Beecroft "Shall I send my slave to England, counsel? Wealthy man that he is, he will feast your princes and yet treat your sovereign with a dignity which, thought she did not deserve it, would yet be given for the honor of my house. Be humble, messenger"

From that schooling came his demand for immediate disavowal of the slave trade. Kosoko would have to fall.

Beecroft had to admit, as he further emptied the whiskey in the captain's cabinet that he had been completely unprepared for the onslaught. He had not seen such starkly royal pride in a black man, even in the two Obas who were awaiting his return in Badagry.

The King had captured the Eletu Odibo, placed him in a casket of brandy, the very sort the British Prime Minister liked to drink, sent it afloat on the lagoon and then, bored with revenge, we had set it ablaze with two precise shots.

His navy had ordered the British off his coast and the HMS Teazer had been pulled off the territorial waters. Foreign Secretary Palmerston was offering trade subsidies but if they would not work, the British would take Lagos right before he left office.

And who would advise him as to the effect? Beecroft, as his wounded pride advised, was no mere messenger. No, he was advisor to the Queen through her Prime Minister through the Minister for Colonies through the Undersecretary for Africa through the Governor of Porto Novo.

"Yes" he reflected aloud to himself "to be a small but important cog in such a vast empire is no mere trifle. No mere trifle"

The captain of the steamer, righteously upset at the official getting gamely drunk on his own excellent whiskey, took this moment to poke his head through the empty windows and ask, in a snidely polite voice if there was anything other than alcohol the counsel wished.

Beecroft ever alert to the concealed hatred of the lower classes towards the aristocracy of whom he was now a temporary member, poured a fresh portion of the whiskey and then regaining the haughty reserve drowned at Lagos, asked "How much further is Badagry?"

"We'll be there within the hour Sire."

"Good. Fetch me a pen and some paper, my good man." The captain turned away upset, in that peculiar stoicism of all bureaucrats which, having been upbraided by some superior was certain to transfer the slight in heavyhandedness to the powerless.

"And keep a bottle -I am sure you have others in cabinet, captain -for my arrival. This is good whiskey and it will help the empire some way. Will it not?"

Captain Joe, dismayed into silence, nodded stiffly and went

on his way to the back of the steamboat where he ordered a black messenger with the same heavyhandedness to stop his flirtations with the cook and provide the counsel with some paper and pen.

Then taking the lad's position astern, in full view of the unhappy cook, the captain considered his unhappy life.

He was one of those men, cursed by destiny, to pursue every invitation and find embarassment at each party. When such men grow into business, they miss the good times of profit as surely as the hands of ladies at balls.

He had come to Africa happy at finally entering the most lucrative trade of the time, the buying and selling of the sons of Ham, but no sooner had he arrived than the British sent the West African Squadron to secure the coastline against the trade.

Then he settled into the pepper trade until such a time as his uncle in the parliament could secure him one final passge to the carribean, a last load of Ham-esians secured at Lagos, but this Akitoye-Kosoko business had slowed such trade.

He was enterprising, this captain; willing to reach the end of the world and return to England prosperous -if only he knew which way to turn, the world being so round and so full of ill-luck.

Now, he stood astern on his own flag-ship while the commissioner drank liquor smuggled from the Americas.

The steersman shouted "Badagry"

"And not a moment sooner" Joe muttered to himself. Badagry was a beautiful town even in a time of thatch roofs but the captain has seen it too often. He continued his self-pity and we may leave him to it.

The commissioner walked out of the cabin at the shout and enjoyed the land approaching them in the unfocused stare of the preoccupied and drunk.

He had begun a letter to Whitehall but shelved it in his waistcoast because, as he reflected, neither alcohol nor anger were proper stimulants to his great duty.

He had every intention of pursuading London to permit him to over-run Lagos. Nothing would give him more joy than to see Kosoko bowing before the messenger.

But as the post left on wednesday, two days hence, he would wait until after he surveyed this beautiful land over which he was sovereign and had a dinner of pork-roast and sat through the congress.

The rememberance of the congress caused such consternation on our drunk royal that the steersman who had been observing him from the corner, from that faith which important personages sometimes inspire in the lowly, asked him if he was well.

"My good man, the cares of this office sit heavy on this poor head" Beecroft said.

The steersman nodded his agreement of the head being presently unable to carry any issue of consequence. "Would you rather I enter the islet two miles down the river?"

"No, no, no. I must make an appearance. Onward, my friend"

From his waistcoast came his great watch. It was six o'clock already, and the anti-slavery congress had been set for four at his residence.

"Good Lord, what is happening to me today? If they must wait, they will. A gentleman may be forgiven this breach when he is as tasked as I am with high affairs of the state"

The consul, thinking thus, went inside and, perusing yesterday's paper, struck the most leisurely pose he could, which was no less magnificent for the lack of witnesses.

At page twelve, the horn sounded balefully and despite himself, Beecroft started. Then he cursed. Then resuming his movement at a more aristocratic pace, the commisioner reached the gang-plank where two of his servants awaited him.

They were wizened, these servants. Even with shaved heads and chin, one would call them grey. And, as Beecroft wryly noted, one could not teach an old dog new tricks.

They did not bow to him as he had instructed them but postrated flat on the ground with each thanking his deity for his Master's safe return just as slaves did in Lagos.

This discomfited the commissioner who had an anti-slavery congress meeting in his house at that moment.

Adedayo and Akanbe, for that were their names, had escaped Lagos to place themselves willingly, willingly was the keyword (I tell you), under his protection.

But he did not expect the fishermen and other on-lookers, having seen him welcomed as an owner rather than fair patron, to understand the fine points between slavery and domestic servitude.

But what would a gentleman do? He walked in-between their fully prostrated form as though he considered their obeisance an indignity worthy of notice.

Dayo and Akanbe promptly jumped up, and fell into a sort of hobbled suppliant gait beside their master, all the while continuing to offer their prayers in respectful hush.

The men proved an example for no sooner had Beecroft entered the town proper than a dozen more hobbled forms attached themselves to him.

They brought court matters, marriage matters, trade matters in prayers addressed to him and his Queen with asides for other dieties. He arrived his home with his English sole confidently striking the earth, his aristocracy fully restored.

The disapproving glance of Ajayi, tending to the bishop under the coconut tree next to the brick-house, did not escape the consul but as he had nothing to do with the matter, he approached the two with his crowd.

The bishop, Reverend Dickson of the Church of England, had his slender body concealed under a great English overcoat.

His little grey eyes shone brightly, and appeared to be, with his grinning mouth, the only part of his face in which any sort of life remained.

Unfortunately, the venerable had a weakness in the legs which forced him to use something scarcely different from a wheelbarrow which Ajayi pushed around.

It was whispered that th Reverend would be soon be recalled and during the last six months of that illness, Ajayi had begun to adopt the patronizing airs and patrimonial tone of those who bear confessions.

It was this same Samuel Ajayi Crowther, whose slight education proved such bliss to the abolitionist proclaiming in London that dark beasts could be trained and who would indeed inherit the bishopric.

But for the moment, he was an altar-boy and with the harshness of new converts, chased the servants and crowd from the presence of God. This left the bishop with Burnsmouth who promptly bent to kiss the hand offered.

"My son", the bishop began in defense of the Ajayi fervently employed in a reenactment of the Saviour with the temple money-changers. The voice was still clear despite the sepulchral look of the fellow "one should always hate sycophants"

Beecroft said "In the matters of God yes. Among men, such sycophants are politically useful"

The bishop nodded in a vague way that gave, instead of his assent, an end to the subject. "What of Lagos?"

The inquiry brought all the humiliation of the afternoon to prominence the consul's mind, and it was again the school-teacher with the livid consternation that throws the whip against a tender back who stood in place of royal Beecroft.

"I gather it did not go well" the Bishop said, and he clucked his regret. The consul, still caught in the swirl of emotions, did not hazard a reply but bowed and retreated.

In that foul mood, the returning Samuel hailed him. "Consul, our Lord Jesus Christ bades us to be humble".

As a messenger, eh? Beecroft thought to himself. He did not condescend to reply but ascended, at a bounce, the three stairs of his verandah into his home.

Now he saw why the bishop had taken residence outside. The parlor, built large -as one befitting a representative of the English sovereign and merchant bribes -was filled to capacity so that there was barely standing room.

He recognized eight other men of the cloak, priests or missionaries of the church missionary society and the catholic church.

He saw, in the corner next to the mahogany table, young Abe and Mister Lyon and Oguze, all liberated slaves who having returned to the land from which they were snatched, promptly engaged in the trade themselves.

They were present as spies, no doubt, for a crises of conscience would not affect such men.

And beside them, in white no less resplendent for the shaded room, sat an officer of the Royal Niger Company. Beecroft recognized him from newspapers as that indefatigable nephew of the great abolitionist, Avery. Good.

The room was indeed crowded but it seemed an invisible line separated those first examined from the next lot who sat in royal grace.

Akitoye, the deposed king of Lagos. Remilekun, his first queen. Two chiefs overdressed in embroidered lace. And the guards standing behind their wicker chairs, six in all, who wore poorly cut french uniforms and looked royal still.

Those next to the mahogany table stood at attention as the consul entered the room and made this cursory examination; and we have already remarked the guards as standing, at ease but watchful.

But the royals did not bother themselves and this would have caused some terrible disagreement considering the insecure mood of the consul had his wife not entered the room that moment by another door.

Perfectly attuned to the temperament and displeasure of Beecroft, and seeing his gaze leave the royals in distate to hers, she caused a diversion.

"Now that he has arrived, I hope none of you will leave us before dinner. The stew is almost ready"

Over the general murmur of eager assent, she continued "but allow a poor wife embrace her husband who runs from one matter of the state to the other. I promise, he will return shortly"

This caused some benevolent chuckling and Beecroft wove a course through the crowd, shaking hands perfunctorily, until he reached her and disappeared into private quarters.

She was a small woman, Mrs Beecroft and suprisingly gay that evening. The moment they entered the master bedroom, she flung herself upon the bed and laughed.

Naturally the consul was disconcerted by all this. But pushing herself up by the arms, Mrs Burnsmouth said "Ah, but we have come a long way from keeping schoolchildren waiting, my dear"

And these words made the weary husband smile. "A long way indeed"

By habit, she approached him. By habit, he sat in the great chair with worn leather which faced the open windows, and accepted her small form into his lap. "I see you are not so happy. What of Lagos?"

"Constance, Lagos is dreadful. There will be no treaty and the King insulted me roundly while rejecting our fair offer

Constance almost leaped from her comfort. "He called you names"

"A mere messenger, he said. And compared me to his slave"

"A mere messenger! A curse on him" she cried. "Was it not for such impertinence that Ham has already been cursed?"

"Even so"

"Well now, you must agree with them in the other room. The time has come for the Englishmen to take their rightful place here -and my husband with them"

"But there is no difference. Did you not see the insolence Akitoye afforded me just now?"

She laughed merrily "And that upset you so, my dear husband?"

"Well, given the events of the afternoon..." he began but his wife put a finger on his lips.

"Do you not know what every servant in Badagry knows? It is not the King but his wife who rules their house. He gives you insolence because of her" She laughed again at his frown. "shall i prove it to you?"

"Well, after dinner, I shall call the queen away and leave you men to it. You will find the poor fellow very self-conscious. He has a healthy view concerning which race is superior. Besides, he is the one looking to regain his throne"

"Indeed. Indeed"

"You had better get to the parlor and I to the kitchen" and the Beecrofts rose.

"Yes, but what to make of all this mess? I fear that if we take Lagos under the flag of these abolitionists, they will push for all sorts of changes. International Slavery is one thing but to abolish it in Lagos itself would render the place ungovernable"

But Constance, who was already at the door, grinned coquettishly at her husband and asked loudly "But what have I to do with all your important state business?" in a manner suggesting that she would advise his letter to London after their visitors had left. She then took the passageway to the kitchen outside and the counsel, crossing the same passage re-entered the room.

His mood suitably recovered, the consul asked if the men of the cloth would allow them refreshments before the women brought in food.

Avery's nephew called out "Our cause is abolitionism, not temperance. We are followers of wilberforce, not John Wesley"

The room erupted into cheers of "Hear, Hear!" and the consul barely had time to lean into the passage and call to Ariyo and Akande for the prized boat liquor and a keg of palmwine, before the tumult, as in all congresses, was turned into a start of business.

"What of Lagos?" a voice cried

"Did that supplanter sign?" came from an african voice which likely belonged to one of the chiefs besides Akitoye

"Will there be peace?"

"Did the King grant you audience?"

To all of these queries from every corner of the room, Burns-mouth gave his aristocratic smile, grateful to be center of some-where.

The wheelbarrow, for that is what we must call that strange contraption locally fashioned as a wheel-chair for his eminence, with the Bishop rolled inside and those closest the door allowed him and Samuel Ajayi room but all eyes remained on the consul.

When he was fully confident of their attention, burnsmouth laid his hands open in the weary manner of resignation "He said No"

The tumult resumed with greater force. There were English-men in the room who naturally disapproved of this disrespect to the English throne and the man who gave it.

There were others more concerned with the slave trade who insulted Kosoko for its continuance.

There were some, like the three former slaves present now as slave-owners, who cursed the Oba of Lagos for very personal reasons. You could notice the pleasure in the royal camp at this turn of affairs.

At this moment, Dayo entered with bottle and jerry-can with Akande behind him carrying almost twenty glasses on a tray balanced precariously on his shaved head.

In such circumstances, each man privately concerned with the safety of the drinking glasses or the heavy burden of Lagos, silence replaced the tumult almost effortlessly.

The liquor and palm-wine were served around to the admir-ation of the men. The priests and missionaries, casting furtive glances at the bottle and again at the wheelbarrow, declined. nor were their fears useless because the peace was promptly broken by that fiery convert behind the bishop.

Perhaps it was merely the fanaticism of new ideas or, as Beecroft darkly thought, an attempt to impress the invalid on whom his promotion hinged.

Ajayi cleared his throat and said "It is ironic that we gather here, with domestic servants, to discuss the case against slavery"

A new stream of that liquid with which the steamboat had acquainted him, was coursing through Burnsmouth and he would rather have held his tongue to savour the drink.

By God, the Americas made such fine whiskey. But he was tired of these Africans carrying the airs which rightfully belonged to his race.

"My friend" he began, without the least friendliness "there is a difference between men such as you who were held in bondage and liberated by men such as gather here, and the men who have placed themselves at my service, running sometimes from the very fate you suffered."

"You think to do me harm by announcing I was a slave. Indeed I was. Indeed I am, even now, slave to our Lord Jesus Christ. And proud of the gospel. But, is this the extent of protection you can offer these men who run to you? To draw you alcohol which you can do well by yourself?"

"Ah, but I see you know nothing of being a gentleman..."

The obstinate Samuel pressed on "So it is the duty of gentlemen to oppose slavery and return to the comfort of servants?"

Beecroft, who was finding himself bested for the second time that day and this in his home, would surely have made an impolitic remark.

A small shadow passed between him and the door-frame and the melodious voice of Constance came again to the rescue.

"What comfort, sire? You think we, who clothe and feed these who have run under our protection, are not burdened by our domestic charges? Would you rather we turned them out into the street? Can the church provide each one with a splendid education and a handsome allowance as it has provided you Sire? And does not our Lord ask us to turn nobody from our door? Is it not just that as we render some small benefit, they give to us too what they can? Shall I then believe you insult us for charity?"

Having successively stammered, given a "I did not say that" and a No, No, Yes, Yes and No to each question posed by the small hostess, the crowd would not allow Samuel speak but collectively offered its apologies to Constance, whose tiny frame shook with annoyance, and her husband.

Mrs Beecroft, whom we have described as surprisingly gay that evening, promtly recovered her smile and said to the crowd "Well, be at ease. I can assure you that the delicacies coming now have been cooked with both my labour and theirs. Samuel, do eat with us"

Cornered, the convert stammered an apology and the triumphant little woman swept into the passageway again.

Beecroft cleared his throat "With such a lovely wife, one need hardly defend himself". The room laughed. "But samuel raises an issue I have wrestled with. Slavery must be stopped indeed. Nobody here denies that fact".

But for three heads, there were vigorous nods of assent. "But if these last bastions of slavery, as my Lord Avery calls Dahomey and Lagos, are conquered, shall we demand no man have a master?"

There was, with the fervency of righteousness, cries of "Yes of course" and "There can be no other way" and "Not one head of the beast left alive" but here, another feminine voice threw the room into silence.

Such voices do not lend themselves to easy description. At once loud and intensely private, commanding and sultry, it was a voice confident of asking men to immolate themselves for the mere promise of a private audience.

It belonged to Remilekun, third wife -and against all custom, Queen -of the deposed Akitoye. She simply said "Let us take this bastion first and these matters will fix themselves" and all the heads promptly agreed the issue as unworthy of discussion.

Not to be outdone, her husband now spoke up "The primary issue is this: what is to be done about Lagos".

To speak after such an agreeable sound in a voice that was too high-pitched for man and royal, and certainly distasteful even in the most boring silence, was an annoyance.

But indeed that was the issue to be faced. The crowd broke into itself, each man taking conference with his neighbour. And all the better since Constance, leading three black women whose red and soaked faces gave the lie to her claim of equal labour, announced dinner.

Mrs Beecroft inherited a disordered room in which no civil meal could be had and had to order, in that sweet but inferior voice, every man to his place.

She took care not to disturb the royals but having set all churchmen on a long bench brought in by Dayo, with their food placed on a long bench brought in by Akande, and having given trays to the others now comfortable seated in chair or wheelbarrow, she called to Remilekun with a smile.

The queen took her time to rise, quite conscious every man had paused his meal to stare at a grace extending beyond her voice.

Constance Beecroft, agile like a mouse, forced her smile and its patience only because she had promised her husband and the two women disappeared into the passageway with the servant-girls in tow.

Taking his cue, the consul took the queen's chair although this was less than prompt since he too had been watching the exit of Remilekun.

We may leave the women who handled themselves so well that neither of the two lost or gained anything by the conversation. Indeed the single highlight was the moment where Remilekun asked constance if she had effected their absence for some reason.

But the English are so well-practiced in prostestations of innocence and the Yoruba in the pretense of belief, that soon they fell into discussion of inanities without losing any warmth. Let us remark in passing that Remilekun was not beautiful.

She was graceful indeed, but there are feline creatures with uneven features and she was of this kind. Her shoulders were too broad, her chin too long, and if one chose the ebony neck for enchantment, there was the disturbing line where the lower end of a slave collar had once pinched.

Her eyes, it must be admitted, were beautiful in their golden brown tint and she had a pleasant gaze which seemed to forget you even while she stared, new in its every look.

This, and that remarkable voice, were her sole redeeming features but were enough to draw both man and woman into the most admiring respect.

Yet the conversation which concerns us remained in the parlor. Upon taking the emptied seat, the consul avidly faced his meal and it was Akitoye who spoke. "Sire, so what is your plan for Lagos?"

How the soul of Beecroft sang to hear that royal call him 'Sire', but the consul, who furrowed his brow and gave the apperance of thought, put the question back to the royal. "What would you do if you were in my shoes?"

"Why Sire, I would look for a man who was already friends with the British and lord over that city and give him the treaty"

"Indeed. but the matter is not so simple since friendships waver. Do they not?"

"Perhaps among the English. My people say '*Aki i ri adie nile ka da agbado fun aja*'. It means 'One does not see chickens about and throw one's corn to the dog' Always direct help where it will be appreciated. Besides I know the British would brook no disappointment. *Adaniloro fagbara koni*"

"And so if you were sovereign..."

"I am sovereign." In Akitoye's mouth, what would have sounded truly royal seemed a shrill pliant "If I were restored to my throne, the treaty would be the first order of business".

The two had carried on as though in private conference but Avery shouted from the end of the room "Well, what do we wait for, then? If we have our man, let us put him on the throne".

This caused no tumult or general agreement because nothing is more indisposed to a revolution of any kind than a full stomach.

But it gathered the crowd into one soul again. Beecroft who kept up his pensive look, was asked by a cleric "surely God has given us the answer. what is this delay?"

Samuel Ajayi answered, seeking penitence now that he had fed. "Matters of state, no doubt. The consul must know things we do not not"

"Matters of state? Bah! Any Englishman who thinks we extend ourselves too far by a concern with Lagos must remember this empire has always paid for itself. Paid with interest, I must say. I am sure Parliament will agree" Avery said.

"Lagos will pay for itself after the slave trade has been ended? No the matter must be done but let us not fool ourselves. This is thankless work"

"Politicians will not concern themselves with charity for no benefit, as my lady Constance said this evening."

Beecroft was incensed "My wife did not say that"

"Implied it then." Avery conceded. "It must be shown that the slaves, once freed can immediately be put to work on rubber and palm-oil plantations. My friends here" and he waved to the creoles beside him, "stand ready to ensure Lagos will be a profitable mission. Indeed it might become the Light to this dark continent when we rid it of this evil"

Bravo, thought Beecroft. Those friends will find credit through Avery and share their profits with the abolitionist.

But he did not have time to pursue the thought because Dayo, his grey head reflecting the lantern when he bowed, whispered news that seemed to surprise the consul

"It appears we have all come to an understanding. Shall we press the cause then? Excuse me" And with that, Beecroft made his way into the passageway.

"Indeed! This evening has been charming, I say. But first I propose a toast. To our man" Avery cried.

It was this salutation of "Our man" which brought Remilekun from her conversation with Constance in the latter's bedroom.

THE CONQUEST

Blood is sacrifice. Everything else in a ritual is substitute for that life-force given to obtain. If one deigns to protect a city from assault, it is blood that is shed -a bull's heart for the warrior, sheep -head for the woman, entire cockerels, preferably black, for each male child and white doves for the pubescent girl.

The priest sprinkles the blood on the owner, calls the Gods to witness, inhales its incense and blesses the devotee. Pours salt and water around the likely thrust of assault. Speaks into the sea at midnight. Heaven can be nowhere it is not bound.

Work is prayer. We toiled deep into the night, arranging the stakes and passilades; the navy was held at the ready, the army only half-asleep, the men of the city facilitated the evacuation. When the eye seemed to droop, hot was passed around.

"Hot" was the name of Seaman Schnapps imported from the dutch countries but so beloved by African Heaven that it became considered its nectar.

It sharpened the eye enough to see and converse with spirits. It granted the favour of the Gods. We drank hot into the night, our talisman glowing, the incisions on our skins recieving charge.

Beecroft had recieved the the assurance of officers that Lagos could be taken almost immediately. Commander Forbes had 300 officers and 200 privates with white blood. Commander wilmot could attach twelve hundred natives to this force. There was the HMS Bloodhound and forty-one boats.

Beecroft gave the order to proceed. He drafted a letter outlying British cause and kept his desk ready to write another. A memo this time. The conquest of Lagos.

No. Conquest would sound too imperialistic for the liberals in parliament. TheLiberation? Irrational. He could a shadow minister mocking the government. His government. The Reduction of Lagos. This was his promotion.

The white man came at dawn, in the overweening confidence of a race willing to let a woman govern them. There were 41 british vessels and a variety of war-canoes.

He brought brown and black faces with him: Gabonese and the Huti. He carried 10 8-pounders and a two-dozen 5 pounders. The flagship sailed under Commander Forbes, a wispy man perceptible to Juju.

Spirits respect contracts. They will go only into the unoccupied or half-full unless they are invited by the domain prefect. A babalawo and a catholic priest are fairly matched, each one a fanatic of an idea but Forbes was light-weight, a consortium of ideas, a patheon with no chain of command. Against such men, Juju enjoys a field day.

Osun gave unsteady seas and the ibeji, eternal twins of mischief, walked the decks as white officers, giving conflicting orders to the natives. There was Sango hurling thunders and afterwards the work of victory was claimed by his cult.

I side with the worshippers of Ogun. There were 5000 men defending Lagos. We were armed with the french muskets and dane-guns and the outrage of free-men. Ogun steeled our hands.

The Bloodhound was under severe cannon fire but a landing party took the beach-head. We let them drive us back. Land. Step upon the ancestral earth. Then Oshodi Tapa cried *"Tani oni Ile yii"*

"Oje tiwa" and we pressed against them, shooting them into the waters, stabbing the floating, the swimming, going into the boats with scimitars and the cry of the defiled. *Ah, Ogun ko fun won ni aye.*

Beecroft and the commander reported three soldiers dead and nineteen wounded but you have seen how treacherous they are.

The Gods had taken a hundred men overboard off British vessels, had broken all the war-canoes, and killed some 400 soldiers. The Gods had defended Lagos with our bodies.

The news got to Palmerston on tuesday the nineteenth and the Foreign Office was furious. Parliament was discussing west african policy and here was an upstart staging a miniature invasion.

But dead britons now roused support for the conquest of Lagos. He instructed the Naval Squadron to take Lagos and install Akitoye. There would be no quarter given. Failure would have heads rolling.

They came again that December. The wounded HMS Bloodhound, the HMS Teaser, a flotilla of boats including The Victoria and the Harlequin, 2000 men and long-range guns.

Oshodi Tapa wanted everything the same way. Odunsi wanted us to deploy the swivel-guns mounted on war-canoes.

"You want to deploy war-canoes against the Naval Power of the world. People who have seen your house and you have not seen theirs?"

"Aki i sa fun ajia ka digbolu eegun. What we are facing is a small force. If we don't destroy it, will we be here to see our own house?"

The council was divided both ways. A land strategy had worked. It suited our strength. There was the adrenaline of november in the memories of the council-room, the charge, the victory. But the equation had changed.

In the end, Kosoko opted for both. "Let us wear them out. Four or five days then we shall send out the navy to attack and harass them.

"It was not a lack of sacrifice. The Gods might have been asleep. Orunmila must have abandoned us.

There was no landing party. Forty boats surrounded Lagos. For three days, the heavy bombardment had struck Lagos, killing thirteen thousand when we stopped the count and sending eight thousand others to the road.

By the fourth day, a shell struck the munitions dump at the palace and caused an explosion loud enough to be heard in Badagry. Our ships were torn apart, the beach-head strewn with the bodies of its defenders.

The guns of the Teazer and the Bloodhound, the Agindigbi, made our cannons a cheap affair. Our muskets were toys, I tell you. We shouted in each ear when it was time to go, time to leave the land to the Gods. It was exile again, this time at Epe.

The British War was over.

MATILDA

And so I returned to Porto Novo. Oba Kosoko and Oba Akitoye -the one in Lagos and the other in the Free State of
Epe -were irrelevant, the British had won. Akitoye's flag
was an incomplete union jack, I tell you.

The swede's network went to them the same way they had
taken Adedibu and the Olushoba. The army would serve their
march against Benin and perhaps against Sokoto. I meant to
serve no-one.

Dahomey was still free. Jose was still alive and the Sacramento was on offer. Matilda was in Porto Novo. I could go into
business and raise a family and it would be nice to travel to England some day to see the queen.

I fancied myself in traditional garb without errand, a slave
holding my totem of Olokun in that christian palace. A rich tourist, free man, messenger of neither court or cathedral, an interpreter of my own soul. It is a fine thing to be altruistic, I tell you,
but Jesus after the crucifixion was handing out commissions on
his behalf.

I arrived rich. The Epe Settlement had given us lands. Kosoko
was the Oloja of Ereko and King of Epe with full tax rights. He
was given an annual pension of 400 pounds and a flag.

Oshodi Tapa was given most of Epetedo and unlimited credit
for a rubber plantation. Osho Akanbi was granted state conces-

sions for his shipping business.

The Idejo chiefs got agricultural subsidies and the ogalade were informed religion would not be taxed. The British committed to an annual donation of three thousand pounds to the Ogboni society. For assimilation, it opened a Freemason lodge.

The slaves had been given manumissions and trading loans. Their children were given free schooling and missionary meals. The 400-strong Oloshoba became the new police with handsome salaries.

The palace offered me my old position as royal chamberlain and I rejected it. Tax Inspector was not good enough either.

I was ordered to disband my small bodyguard, a hundred pounds per head, and I sent them, reluctant free-men, to Porto Novo and Matilda.

The palace then granted me Epe-Oni; I promptly resold half to a British agent, the CMS missionary Thomas, for a church and school.

The other half, with its villa, I sold to the newly arrived son-in-law of Beecroft. I sold half the navy to fulani merchants and built a brief career as arms-dealer in the Egba-Remo War.

I was called immoral and I fancied myself great, I tell you, because it is the term for the man who answers nothing other than his own conscience, desires his own will.

I justified all my actions. The gods had failed us which meant they had converted to Jehovah or were beaten -we might as well become Christains. The boats and guns were lying useless.

Besides, Ikorodu -a Remo township -was just north of Lagos. The British and Akitoye were concerned, Epe could be next, profits could be made. I was patriot, friend and merchant.

I was called immoral but Lagos was changing. The palace could only collect market tax and the Consulate decided how much. The Slave trade was over, the baracoons cemented anew held palm-oil or rubber.

There was a bible everywhere and guns only with the British, the Safo, and registered members of the hunter's guild. What good would the palace do me?

Perhaps that was the immoral thing. To question benefit for self, not community nor royalty nor divinity.

I had amassed a fortune greater than Osinlokun and was not as generous as the old man. I entered Porto Novo with fifteen thousand pounds and the curses of all Lagos.

I could marry Matilda and we would move into the house in which we first made love. I had ordered two bedrooms knocked down for a ball-room fit for Lord and Lady. A stable was under construction. The Arabesola garden was to be expanded.

When the ship docked, my personal guard marched up with much fanfare. The port paused and I gave hundreds of pounds in answer to their curiosity. Yes, a private sovereign had arrived.

This was no vanity, I tell you. It would be a good thing for Gezo to hear of my arrival -a rich man would find land and women for free.

Matilda would have ladies-in-waiting. With a title I could keep slaves upon free black land, perhaps plant cotton.

I rode a fine horse while my men marched on both sides and the spectators blocked traffic. I was polite, visiting the parson, inviting the merchants, donating to the missionary orphanage - all before dusk.

I sent gifts -an ornate sword and thirty bags of pepper to the local official, the Wey of Porto Novo. Let him hear.

Then I arrived home to Matilda, the beautiful Matilda. She had bought a turkish rug, told me no one had ever walked it and I must as owner and sovereign. "Oba wa, eyi ni aafin re"

I walked the earth as though I had a right to it. There were servants and guards on both sides and Matilda on the stairs. It was a long way from a tryst in the guardroom.

"Matilda, iyawo mi"

"Oko mi, oba mi"

I stretched hands to give her a hug and she plunged a dagger into my heart.

I remember the pain soon overwhelmed by confusion. *Was this a dream*? I stared down at the dagger. Surely a dream. It looked familiar. A knight on the hilt.

The Olusoba dagger I had given her. She said she wanted nothing to do with a traitor so there it was -a gift from the heart and into it. A dream. A fountain.

She was crying and cursing me, bidding the ancestors refuse me, sending my spirit on endless errand as sea-wraith.

They stood there, the guards and servants stood, as I crumpled onto the opulence of imported turkish rug. I remember seeing the condemnation in their eyes. I had lost them Lagos. Something never mine to begin with.

ABIKU

JP Clark

Coming and going these several seasons,
Do stay out on the baobab tree
Follow where you please your kindred spirits

If indoors is not enough for you
True, it leaks through the thatch
When floods brim the banks,
And the bats and owls
Often tear in at night through the eaves
And at hamattan, the bamboo walls

Are ready tinder for the fire
That dries the fresh fish up on the rack.
Still its been the healthy stock
To several fingers, to many more will be
Who reach to the sun.
No longer then bestride the threshold
But step in and stay
For good. We know the knife scars
Serrating down your back and front
Like beak of the sword-fish,

And both your ears notched
As a bondsman to this house
Are all relics of your first comings.

Then step in, step in and stay
For her body is tired,
Tired, her milk going sour
Where many more mouths gladden the heart.

REPUBLIC

Regnabo

CEREMONY

Thunder clap.

Independence Day. The British said they granted it and the nationalists swore they earned it but that friday afternoon at the Lagos race-course was an accident of history giving the lie to both.

It did not stop the celebrations. The shouts reached past the market, past the movie-house and post office, and into the offices of the Ministry of Information where I worked.

It was in the streets when you looked down and came into the office with the unimaginative combinations of new national colours.

We had been given the day off but we showed up to put in a half-day of work. We were proud to be civil servants, we were educated, offspring of the British, heirs to this new nation, the machinery of its government and we would be damned to abandon our ethics for a mere change in guard.

Also the flat felt dreary and the day stretched like an interminable desert before me so I had dressed up to push some papers which could wait, and -with the way we each avoided the other's gaze -I was not the only one.

We worked until lunch hour when the sun was overhead and the noise loudest and then everybody packed their bags as though to say sufficent duty had been done. In groups of three or four, the office emptied into the race-course. I and Vera joined Pius in his beetle.

The race-course had been ceded by King Decemo, son of Akintola, to the British in 1857 because it was decided that the new administration could not function at maximum colonialism without cricket and horses and hockey.

It resembled an airport terminal and could hold fifty thousand persons. It had never done so until this afternoon.

Lagos was there. The homeless, the pickpocket, the day-business man and night-shift women, the market-women, sailors, clergy, the budding literati, the Lagos that came out at night in the corners of the colony and left broken teeth in its wake.

Everyone was there. On foot, bicycles and cars. Our beetle wound its way through the stream of nationhood.

We had to park two miles away and the crowd pressed against us even there, draining what little enthusiasm was left. Pius wanted us to go to the Hotel Avey to eat, but I had no money and was ashamed to say so.

"I'll come join you guys. I want to catch this scene"

Vera wanted to say something but Pius jumped in "You want my keys"

"No, I'll be fine." I looked around meaningfully "Might get lost. If I'm not back in an hour, we see tomorrow?"

He nodded with gratitude. Vera had understood. "Bye Pete" she said.

My wave was limp. I turned away with sudden loneliness. I liked Vera. Vera liked cars. I turned towards the race course.

There were children in the large road, pot-bellied and dirty and waving green-white-greens glued onto straws. There were women, some hawking and some beating the children and some filled with that purposeless euphoria walking them about.

The men were on the street corners or in the pubs or struggling like me towards the race-course with a face contemplating the national destiny and a sweat-soaked newspaper beneath their arm. But it is always the young women who catches one's eye.

The African woman is a fine specimen of arrant lust. Civil servant joke was slavery was only an excuse for the white man to re-enter paradise.

Paradise wore sun-dresses, large wrappers, stark burqas - this temptation was not purposeful -but the body stretched and beckoned. In the dog-heat of the African noon, their tilting laughter and swaying hips were a different sort of hope.

I met her at the gates. A girl was against me, pushing past me, rude like the green coat and green scarf and everything else she wore. I would let it go.

"Hello Honey" she said to me, her eyes smiling "want to buy me a drink?"

Well, here is your woman, Pete. Here is your woman. Smile and act sauve. Instead I avoided her gaze and muttered "no thanks". Shame on you Pete. But I was not ashamed. She had wanted me.

The battle at the gates was no disrespect, after all, but the desperate search of attention from a civil servant on the rise.

Yes, independence meant something. Freedom would mean more pay, more ease -enough with these unafrican ethics -there could be a warm body next to mine and I could see her soft belly and full breasts. I wondered, idly, if her underwear too was green. I turned and walked back towards her.

She saw me and smiled. I forced myself to look into her eyes, beyond the hypocrisy of liberty -she was counting how much

I was worth. "Hello darling. Changed your mind about that drink?"

"What's your name?"

She laughed. She gave her name. I never remembered it until the end. I called her Green and it stuck, and we laughed and talked of Nigeria. A student at Uni-Ibadan. A Biologist. The drinks arrived from a push-cart and we went on with racing heart-beats.

She had this fond style, parting her hair and looking at me with a "Oh, but isnt it beautiful? Isn't it" She thought a baloon, the fine cars, the sun was beautiful. She made me feel charming. I was charming, I tell you.

Then it happened. The Captain came through the gates too and on his arm was another version of Green. Wide-eyed inno-cence with western possibilities. Laughter and a "darling"

The Captain was just as jovial. He tipped the pushcart lady and turned to me "Say mate, why don't we have a double date. Let's get out of here. What do you think?"

I thought the british accent a bit too thick. I thought this thing wasn't a date. I thought I would say No because I might run into Pius and Vera. Vera. "Sure. Okay. Where are we headed?"

Green spoke before the captain could "Oh, but isnt it beauti-ful, pete? Isn't it" She could have been talking of her drink, the uniform, the outing.

The captain laughed at my shadow of annoyance "Well, as the lady says, it is beautiful. May I suggest the Hotel Avey. Its just two streets away. "

Well, that suited me just fine. The captain gave me a small flask and I drank hot schnapps. Arm in arm, we four walked back through the gates.

We were laughing in the heat, walking through the middle of

the road with "excuse mes" and the liberty of this fine national day. We shared the flask often. The team spirit.

I did not run into Vera. I did not care. We shared our names. We danced that night. We sang the new national anthem. *Nigeria we hail thee. Our own dear native land.* The lobby rose with lusty throats. The hotel gave free drinks. We wept at midnight.

I think the clientele walked to their cars or homes with their spines a little straighter. Martin Luther King Jr. may have been there.

Three years later, he was crying *"Free at last, Free at last, Thank God Almighty we are free at last"*. It was our whisper that night, I tell you.

"She's an awfully charming girl". The women had gone to the bathroom. They had seen it in the movies. You powdered your nose and stayed fresh. I wondered if he was talking of his or mine and decided not to pursue the subject.

"Yes, she is"

"Will you marry her"

I laughed "I met her at the race-course"

"What? Then you must marry her. Such synergy"

"Will you marry her?" I returned.

"I might. My Father will tell you I am the most irrational man alive"

"Why?"

He seemed distracted for a moment. "What do you think will happen? Now that we have Nigeria?"

"A little trouble with the politicians. A little trouble with Britain. After that we coast along. Nothing major, I tell you"

He smiled "Are you blocking my promotion?"

"Get out" Alcohol is a strange thing. Friendship too. I was telling a soldier get out and we were laughing in that lobby of Avey.

"I think it would be bad. Look at India and Pakistan. The British should have done the same thing here"

"And undo their creation? Largest black nation is a big thing for them. Gives them something to rub in french faces" I gave it some thought "I don't think it will be bad at all. Unity in diversity, you know"

"Yes but religion is not language. The north has imperial islam, and the south has evangelism" He had a way with words. "What if something comes up, something like Sharia, like the issue of slavery in the American states? Something abhorrent to certain people but a way of life for another?"

"You certainly the pessimist"

He laughed. "Realist" and he would have said more but the ladies with new powder were back at the table and asking what we were talking about. We demurred and Green, my green, said "Men and Politics"

I thought about the marriage thing. She was beautiful. Slender until the waist and yes we had hit it right. I liked her and I liked myself with her. An awfully charming girl, alright. She saw me looking at her and made a face; I laughed, gave a mock frown to the opposite couple applauding our little drama. The captain winked. Green slid up to me with the scent of vanilla and pressed herself against my arm.

The Captain drummed the table. "Okay, what say we get out of here? I need to be up at 5am"

"The night is still young" The other Green said.

"No, let's go. What you say, mate?"

It occured to me that he was a man accustomed to command and his questions were very polite orders. "Yes, Let's"

The lobby was getting empty anyway. It was a sort of new year's eve for us and the people had done the ritual.

They could sleep now and wake up Nigerians. The disc jockey had closed and the music was now set to the National Anthem. The bartenders were cleaning the glasses. "Come on Green. Captain, you ready?"

"Always, Chap"

The Captain drove a beautiful mercedes. When we walked through the streets and into the car, Green whistled. He called it a gift. His Green purred. I consoled myself that I was a man of integrity. No way that car was bought on an army salary.

"Would you like to give her a spin, my friend?"

"Who me?" The spirit was receding and I found myself on thin ice. These army men.

"Yes, you. Come on. Come on, take it"

I took it. He made me drive to my quarters first and Green was in the seat next to me with a "Oh, but Peters, isnt beautiful. Oh Darling" as I drove the finest car down the now empty streets.

Sometime in the night we had exchanged cards. Certain men impress you with the assurance that life will never be the same. I would confirm it years hence.

He was not a spendthrift in anything but his youthful laugh. He was a fine man with his military cut, nothing like a soldier on a paltry allowance and he simply laughed when he caught me staring at him unabashedly through the rear-view.

We dropped off at my house. He took his vehicle and his girl, had I and Green standing on the verandah of my flat and left with a "Say mate, what say we do this next weekend? Lady" and a wave.

I imagine I looked as grateful as Pius.

1960

We were meant to sleep that fine night of october thirty-first; sleep after the street-parties and toasts, our eyelids coated green and white and green above, a vague Nigerian dream beneath. We were meant to rise up the next day reborn.

When it did not happen, it was agreed that parliament was only just begun and the miracles would flood the nation in a month. This too failed, mostly because the art of governance needed some hundred days for comprehension.

Then it was a year, something sufficient and definite to wipe off british fingerprints, to find the dividends, to celebrate again.

Afterwards, because of John Kennedy, we were told to shrug off our colonial expectancy and to think as citizens of what we could do for the fatherland. There would be no reprieve.

To be fair, those were strange times. French pride, surprisingly sustained after vendee, found its grave in the Algerian desert. The Americans were finding this superpower thing a fragile sham in vietnam, in cuba.

Kennedy, adonis-faced kennedy, was a fine compliment to that tide of hope rising across the African Continent.

Space was open, with Yuri and John Glenn and Armstrong up there and Gary Powers detained somewhere down here.

The Russians were in Africa, besotted with these pitifully primitive communities which had no Marx and yet had a thesis of communal property.

It was the age of the Hydrogen bomb, with the russians, brits, french and chinese celebrating bar mitzvahs one after the other.

It was the birth of the contraceptive pill, the summer of love and drugs, the launch of the feminine mystique.

There was John Steinbeck as literary giant that decade and Cassius Clay for black sport. There were altars to Elvis and Bob Dylan, and children watched the flintstones.

And there was Marilyn Monroe, that soulful canvass with little dot. Elizabeth Taylor, Audrey Hepburn, and Sharon Tate wanted at the movies and forgotten in black nymphs.

Music lived in rich homes with mahogany turntables. More homes had televisions. Media was international and a world once mired in local gossip, now found itself nodding to the left and right in perfect cadence.

It was the age of assasinations. There was Martin Luther King on the cover of Time's Magazine. There was the lifeless body of Malcolm X on the stage of the Audubon Ballroom.

Patrice Lumumba would face a firing squad, sylvanus Olympio and Rafael Trujillo and Jason Sendwe would follow suit. Hendrik Verwoerd would die. And Kennedy, the poor kennedys.

It was the age of opposition. The Military-Industrial complex versus sovereign man. Capitalism and Communism.

Psycho-analysis against common-sense. Man versus Woman. White and Black in tug-of-war. There was India and Pakistan, Isreal and the Arabs, Ireland and Britain, China with itself.

It was the age of assertion with the portuguese harried in Angola and Mozambique and Guinea. 32 countries found independence and more would follow. There was Harold Macmillan, that old man, apt representative of the British Empire returning to its childhood.

The civil rights movement won grounds, the anti-war movement harried governments addicted to war. The United Nations asserted parental concern, assented to neo-imperialism.

In Nigeria, three men held the reins of our times: Ahmadu Bello, Nnamdi Azikiwe and Obafemi Awolowo and each pulled the horse to his home.

The Queen of England had left us a country with a large northern region, an educated west and capitalist east under these leaders. Not a nationalist stood among them. Feudalism, Pan-Africanism and Socialism were the quiet topics of the day.

It now fell to the census to decide who would hold the parliament and all the regions found the opportunity too great to resist.

The south counted families twice and the North counted a village's herd. Travellers and passers-by were counted and no, it did not matter if you passed often. When all else failed, the census officers were gifted prophecy by regional edicts and counted the unborn.

In the West, population had jumped by seventy percent, and in the East, by some strange level of fecundity never seen before or repeated since, there was an increase of 120 percent in ten years.

Somehow the North came out ahead, suddenly discovering some eight million northerners who must have been asleep. They were accused of cheating. When the legal noise died, Bello still held the court.

His proxies now sought to cripple the opposition by removing it from regional power. There were rumours and counter-rumours in the west.

A party split. A steady beat of local violence. Everybody laughed it off; Awolowo had it coming after all. A strategist had been outmanoeuvred.

This was the age of Nigerian communism and the coker commission and the Akintola about-face. The Federal Government began a fire in the western region, invited itself in and locked everyone else out by emergency powers.

Awo's complaint was treason, another region was carved out the west and granted to Zik, the North remained in power.

The opposition was ended and this was all politics, I tell you. Statecraft took a long time to master but the game of immediate advantage was easy to learn.

Labor saw. All the unions came together and formed the Joint Action Committee. The Government ignored it. The strike which followed ground the economy.

The Government called a committee, the committee called for evidence, the evidence called for a comprehensive report which counselled patience with the government.

Labour marched singing *"Ta lo ni ile yi?"*. Who owns this land? Who owns this land?

"Awa lo nile yi"

They marched to the race course where the flag had triumphed in 1960 but this time they met batons, tear-gas and punches.

Ta lo ni ile yi? The Federal Government does.

The threat of federal aid became blunt. Federal security became partisan. When the 1964 elections came, the opposition were denied both.

Intimidation was rife and boycotts of the election were not widespread enough to be effective. It took 1964 for us to realize this was no democracy.

And that was the age, I tell you. Politicians were feared and hated. They were boys playing police and robbers with live ammunition.

We called upon the Army, petitioned the British, prayed to God Almighty. Perhaps the response came backwards but the first answered on the 15th of Januray 1966.

KHAKI

In the name of the Supreme Council of the Revolution of the Nigerian Armed Forces, I declare Martial Law over the Northern Provinces of Nigeria. The Constitution is suspended and the regional government and elected assemblies are hereby dissolved.

All political, cultural, tribal, and trade union activities, together with all demonstrations, and unathorised gatherings, excluding religious worship, are banned until further notice.

The aim of the Revolutionary Council is to establish a strong united and prosperous nation, free from corruption and internal strife. Our method of achieving this is strictly military but we have no doubt that every Nigerian will give us maximum cooperation by assisting the regime and not disturbing the peace during the slight changes that are taking place.

We laughed at "slight changes".

The young military officer who read the speech, Major Chukwuma Kaduna Nzeogwu was confused. He had done good work but Major Emmanuel Arinze Ifeajuna, chief coup plotter, had failed to destroy Army High Command. Lagos had not fallen.

But at the time we thought it was a sense of humor. The Sarduana of Sokoto, the Prime Minister of the Federal Republic and Festus Okotie-Eboh, finance minister and most corrupt man in Nigeria were murdered. Slight changes.

The General Officer Commanding was said to be in talks with brilliant Major to prevent the latter marching upon Lagos.

Nzeogwu was dark and lean. He spoke quietly with a sardonic glance. He had believed in Nigeria and chose to believe it again by handing himself over to Ironsi.

The latter would imprison him contrary to agreements and in six months they would both be dead. But in that moment, we felt it was humour and 1960 again, this time with martial music. All the doors were open.

The private offices were empty and the senior civil servants were crowded around the conference table, fraternizing with janitor and sundry.

There were cakes on the table, small pies with a lot of sugar found in any lagos store -someone had brought in packs in a hurry and a couple had fallen at the door -and bottles of cocacola and a chalet passed about not-so-discreetly.

The manager of my department, Mrs Efe watched me walk in and hugged me with the surest maternal affection.

Mrs Efe, whose haughty demeanour had given her the nickname "Medusa", who was now laughing at my face contorted with the visceral trauma of a brain turning upon itself.

She had done it to every member of her department. It made one want to drink, it made the coup personal.

Nobody knew anything so they claimed to know everything. Yes, every corrupt soul had died in this cleansing gun-fire.

There were British commandos behind this. People whispered in groups that their cousion or uncle, a fine soldier, had been dropping hints about this for weeks.

People back-slapped and laughed over the silly innuendos; Someone intoned a prayer for the great Nigerian military, second only in organization and discipline to the even finer Federal Civil Service.

There was Amen and wine. The bespectacled spoke of the direct implications: an invasion of our neighbours, the end of french influence, the creation of the first true pan-african union.

A man's wife mirror had broken two days ago and he had told his wife Nigeria would soon have a coup -Wait, he would call her now; *wait, are you doubting me?*

In a few weeks, the bonhomie I met on January 16th would be replaced by mutual suspicion, the jubilation by sheer terror.

We closed and found pockets of soldiers on the streets and crowds at the newspaper stands. Nobody truly knew what had happened still.

There was fighting between the army, we were told. There were roadblocks and checkpoints. The mutiny had been set down, it had succeeded, it was not a mutiny, it was non-existent. Conflicting reports came from relatives in Kaduna, Ibadan, Enugu.

I dropped off the bus and the Tourist cafe was the same way. That was a good thing. People were talking about the coup but it was muted, the sort of thing one did not discuss in public, an indecency until one could tell how it affected one.

The café was in a squat one-story brick building with the Ketu's cheapest apartments upstairs and a seedy newspaper next-door.

Both were run by the octogenarian Potters, Big Mac and Sotto his wife. It was a building long past youth, and the torn leather chairs inside were matched with tables losing the edges of their Formica.

It was a torment, midday, because of non-functional fans and the naked 200 watt bulbs scattered on the inside; but at evening, when the wind came up from the coast and the dirty windows and double-doors were opened wide, one could drink terrible coffee or miserable food with some measure of self-respect.

The proprietors found each other as repulsive as the town found their businesses and they would often hurl insults at each other across the dilapidated interior.

In spite of all this, or perhaps because of the disagreeable air which pursued other customers, the small-town artists had declared the Café their turf and every evening, one was bound to find people who needed the customary quiet: writers, painters, chess-players, shy teenage couples and the occasional misguided visitor to town.

My work at the Ministry of Information required me to have multiple ID Cards and I had the personas to match. I mingled with the Cafe crowd often. Not today.

Sideways, the printing press ground out the weekly, providing a low background hum for the music of the place, punctuated every twelve minutes by the vehement voices of the potters. I went through the cafe and entered the yard.

The yard was a square with a dirty well in its middle. It held thirty-six studio apartments and eight flats stuck in the middle of each row.

I let myself into the cold and dreary place and headed to the balcony for a smoke. I knew how such things ended but every evening I convinced myself it would be different; it never was.

Lagos was a callous place, crude like jagged granite and you could let it go or lie on it but nobody was changing for you and the city was older than you and *who be you sef*?

There was the unspoken agreement among neighbours that I will tolerate your moderately loud music, your late-night gatherings, the particularly loud girlfriend, the cries of your children and errant farts of your obese wife, and you will tolerate mine.

This was a city and it was the same anywhere on the planet where people had to live in such close quarters.

But there was also Lagos: under no circumstance were you to help a neighbour, to look at him kindly, or to de-escalate the conflict bound to begin from the first day of your lease.

Place the I-Pass-My-Neighbour generator as close to his door as will not provoke a fistfight. Work harder; you need money for fuel to leave your generator on into early hours so he steps out at dawn with the PTSD of this war-zone.

If his prayers work and your stereo is destroyed by NEPA, well, kill cockroaches loudly at four AM. Never give in. Never, never, never give in.

My neighbours, a inter-tribal couple with three kids and a house-help, crammed into one apartment had argument for their weapon.

They argued about everything, including the rules of arguments. Smelling socks from the man's day, and the flies which came with the woman's dry fish, and the children beaten and coaxed and used as weapon by each parent.

The man was in night-school and had no time, *honey I have no time*, for the stupid night prayers conducted so loudly that the Devil not only left her family alone but the compound and perhaps the street.

That night, while I smoked, the argument was about the maid, a nubile yoruba girl who had suddenly stopped wearing pant.

"You dey defend am. Only God knows wetin you dey do when I no dey"

"When you no dey....which one be...me wey dey work morning to night, dey go school, by the time I don reach house you dey here with your dirty fish. You dey crase?"

"Na you dey crase. Thunder fire you. You no go see that fish for your soup again. Make I ask you: the time you dey reach house for afternoon nko? You dey always forget something for house, *Oniranu*. I go con come back, meet this *odaju-eyan* wey dey stink of lust and she no dey ever wear pant. Why you no go defend am?"

"You no get sense. You you dey wear pant for inside house?"

"Eh, you go like make e dey easy na"

"I go slap you o. Wetin dey worry you? You go use that your dirty mouth talk this thing and e go soon happen, e go happen I swear, as you no wan get sense"

"Try am if I no go cut that thing..."

I threw my cigarette and went in to the second-hand gramophone. Records were expensive and I was in no mood for the cracking version of Beatles but anything, anything to drown out the noise. It always ended the same way.

The man would storm out, the woman would mutter loudly for an hour, then the man would return and send the children outside

"I see una friends downstairs o, make una go play" and the grateful children would stumble downstairs and the house-girl with them, and the man would drag his wife gently "come eee, you dey like misbehave"

And she would say "why I no go misbehave" but it would be said gently, a conditional apology.

Shortly afterwards, I would be subjected to strong odor mixed in with fish and socks, and there would be peace when the children returned, peace until her night prayers.

In three weeks, the igbo man would be hounded out the compound by a mob of machete-weilding fulani. I do not think he ever saw his wife again.

Green came in on Beatle's "*Yesterday*"

I had poured myself some seaman schnapps and was back to balcony and cigarettes, asking myself why Juju had not stopped the British from enslaving some fifty million Nigerian people and their millions of ancestors and fifteen centuries of withcraft.

Green. She wanted to get married on your fifteen pounds a month salary, had forced you to attend her church some days where you were assured he who found a good wife had found a good thing.

Green. She brought in alot of money these days and you were afraid to ask.

She spoke of her sister who just got married last month and this friend who was getting engaged in a month, the boyfriend -such a romantic -had set it up with them, the committee of friends and

"Peters, peters, don't you think a public engagement is such a beautiful thing? Makes everybody know just how serious you are"

I said No. "Things are hard in this country. Wise people cut down costs and just get married quietly"

"My village people would not even let us rest. A civil servant is a big thing o" She paused "Is it the money? I can..."

"So I should spend my annual salary because of your village people? And no, I am not touching your money"

She thought for a bit, then resumed the smile and repeated that she was truly in earnest and why, "If my darling decides we should do things quietly, that is what we should do. I ought to submit. And it is our money, darling"

She kissed me, thought for a bit more and then asked me "Am I submissive"

"Yes, Green"

"And do you love me like Christ loves the church?"

"Yes Green"

"Am I your one and only?"

And that is the last thing I remember of that night because afterwards my mind was burdened by the tension of those days, burdened into amnesia or a jumble.

Next thing, Green was there, on that same balcony but perhaps another night, telling me "Peters, Peters, don't you think a second coup is beautiful thing?"

Aguiyi Ironsi was missing, perhaps dead and Yakubu Gowon had taken the chair. The progrom against the Igbos had begun in Kaduna -some thirty thousand murdered by neighbours they had known all their life.

We saw the maimed, the heartbroken, the bankrupt trooping into Lagos. We saw the girls raped into catatonic state, the bruised and the naked.

In Lagos, we saw igbo soldiers killed by fellow-officers, we saw men jumping into civilian clothes, female dress, to avoid the ethnic cleansing.

We heard of executions at the airport, the sea-ports, the car-parks of the federal civil service. Everybody moved circumspectly for death was in the hands of these drug-addled soldiers.

They called it the July Re-match where the North wrecked violence against the East for the first coup, the igbo coup, the attempt to control the nation by nyamiri.

"Peters, Peters, don't you think this pregnancy is a beautiful thing?"

This was the wrong time to get pregnant. One didn't know if a child would be born Nigerian or something else or stateless, so violent was the rage.

There were burning tires on the road, there were vehicles and houses with windows smashed, and up North a mob had attacked an Igbo-owned hospital and broken the heads of babies, torn pregnant bellies open, raped the sick into death.

This was the wrong time to get pregnant but "a child is a gift from God" and family planning was of the devil. I don't know if it was Green or Vera telling me this.

The always sunny Vera and her pensive face and then she disappeared. From memory and office and life. People disappeared alot those days.

And then there was Pius, drunk and crying shameless at my balcony, he didn't know where his fiancee was and he was running back East.

He didn't say it but fear fought with doubt; was Vera dead or one of the girls who now flocked to the barracks to earn a protector and lived large, comparatively safe lives under the caressing protection of the new heirs of Nigeria.

He disappeared too, to village or a mass-grave and I never found him, despite earnest efforts, when I returned to the East.

I returned to the east, I tell you. It would have been a foolhardy thing to remain in the lagos of 1967.

It was no place for the strange and when we heard of white men assaulted, with the sincerest apologies of the Nigerian Government, I was certain my looks would not defend me for long.

A single consideration of my international passport could

have me constricted by two tires and drenched in a gallon of petrol and cleansed from a fulani earth.

Because I was East, there were no academic distinctions to be had about the Igbo tribe. If you lived down the coast, close to the Niger Delta, you were Igbo, minority talk be damned and what, pray tell, was dual citizenship? Nobody was looking at passports. I looked half Nyamiri.

I returned to the East but first I had to find a way to tell Green in a way she would be enthusiatic, and this was easy because she knew Ojukwu. He needed help and it seemed that I could help him.

"Oh you mean like help out with the relief efforts?"

"Maybe"

"You would be a soldier if war comes, won't you Pete"

"I might enlist, yes"

"You must enlist, Pete. I think of that peaceful first night. 1960. The day I met you. These days are so terrible but the Captain would make everything right, won't he?"

I assured her he would. I puffed my cigarette. "He's a colonel now"

"Oh but isn't that beautiful Pete, isn't it?"

I assured her it was. We kept quiet for a while, smoking into the burning night, and then she turned to me fiercely "Remember you are a father now. Don't go die. You have a duty to your friend but also to your unborn son"

"Green..."

"I know what you want to say, how a woman ought not to concern herself with man business but you know I love you so and we will get married and have this beautiful baby. The Captain doesn't like war, I know that but..."

"Colonel" I was being peevish on purpose.

She glared at me. "He'll always be our Captain" The glare died into loneliness. She looked like a waif on the balcony, her cigarette dangling off absent-minded fingers. "When are you going?"

"Tomorrow".

She wept.

EXODUS

I chose the road. There were mammy-wagons heading East, running into Asaba and across the Niger Bridge into Anambra and I clambered into one the dawn of the sixth.

At my feet there was a small child who had gotten separated from his family but he had been put here by good samaritan hands in the belief that anywhere East was better than the mob-infested corners of Lagos.

I took him for a companion , sharing bread and drink with him for so many days that when he was discovered by his mother and taken away into a new vehicle, I felt a deep sense of bereavement. It was good thing we were already on eastern soil.

What were we running from? Yes, Igbo officers had been slaughtered and a few bigwigs had found their names on the purge-list but what were we, child and mother and me, trying to escape so quickly so hard that our convoy, some four hundred and fifty mammy-wagons, blocked the roads and worked 350 miles into four days?

For that matter, what was I running from? I did not look Igbo to the practiced eye, spoke nine nigerian languages and could convince anyone of my south african heritage. What was I running from?

I had left job and house, both reasonably secure for me because it was no longer reasonably secure for people like me.

There was a faint terror that the questioning looks, the un-ashamed perusal by federal civil servants, could change so easily into the crudity of hausa gangs unlikely to make distinctions.

There was the fear, far-fetched though it seem, that I would be asked to prove my loyalty by butchering my own people.

Not that they were my people but other people thought them so and that made it so. At this time the denial of war was mad-ness.

But it was not merely a running away from. We were going *home*, whatever that meant, and the steely grimaces of the young men made it certain these were not cowards but pioneers.

The igbos had spread into the deserts of the North and into the rainforests of yorubaland in the belief of One Nigeria. They were content to leave political power where it lay, to pay a bit more tax, to be kept outside the towns.

They had carried their Chi with them, sometimes along with Jesus Christ, and kept themselves separate. They had made money or bureaucratic connections, making it easy for their tribesmen to join them and their children to build. For these sins, they were now chased out of Nigeria and there was the feel-ing the country would regret it.

For the moment I was the one regretting it. I had never been much good without duty. A place to go, a person to go to, instruc-tions to follow. My life was wrenched from its ten year plan into the unknown now and an uncertainty of radio channels.

I could have gone to the airport, found a new job, some comfortable structure sure to induce amnesia. But there was the captain and the carefree face in that rear-view mirror of a merce-des on a distant night.

"Oya, dey jump down one by one. Everybody go chop. Just jump down jeje, then join that line wey dey there. Wait. I say,

Wait"

The police sergeant jumped out just in time before the mass of humanity poured down from the mammy-wagon.

We were no different from the other trucks. People were tired. Happy to be home. Exhuasted with authority. We wanted a piece of bread and some sunlight.

I stretched my legs on Igbo soil. So this was Onitsha, largest market in West Africa now transformed to a relief camp.

Priests and police tried to organize the people into sections for the soup kitchen but it was an impatient mess. The music of its air were the cries of hungry children and the wailings of the bereft.

I registered my name as a correspondent and joined another bus. I chose Felix's house at Enugu.

He had been an old class-mate in university days, the sort of man who respected your distance because he kept one himself. I went to his Wuthering Heights and after the reminiscence, we resumed our habitual sneer of inconvenience.

I slept on the couch the first three nights, rising only to use the toilet, fetch water down the road and buy food items from peddlers. There were no markets anymore, Felix told me. "Looting is at an all time high."

I told him I knew Ojukwu.

"Everyone knows Ojukwu."

"No, he is a close acquintance"

"Okay"

I did not like being disbelieved. "I am going to his office tomorrow"

"Goodluck"

"Where is it?"

He laughed "The telephone? Over there in the corner. Call your bosom friend and ask his address"

I was too tired to argue. "Where's your wife?"

He looked confused a moment, then looked at the wedding band on his finger "Oh this? I can't stand a wife. I wear it to keep women away"

"I thought she was your wife"

"Who?" He had a house-servant who cleaned the house wednesday evenings while he walked the dog. I do not know if they had an agreement that she never say a word and thus despoil his personal space or if she was merely reticent but I had recieved a "Good evening" and silence to my conversation all through yesterday evening. Was an intelligent soliloquy.

"Chiasoka? No o" And with that he returned to his book.

I decided I would walk. He asked to not walk too far. "For safety but you'll also need those legs for your state visit"

I ignored his laughter and strolled down the street. Men like Felix are such pleasant company if one does not spend time with them.

I wanted conversation and the place to find it would be a beer-parlor. The best would always be found around those artefacts of colonialism: the post office, the railways, secretariats, the parishes, the museum itself.

Beer-palours had always been the Nigerian town-hall. It had been the centre of independence with arguments lasting long into the night, the saloon of the educated and soap-box for the political wannabe.

The Madame moderated conversations and reserved sole right to send out any contestant when the heat of alcohol and discourse threatened violence.

It was in our beer-parlours that the nationalists had preached to the masses, first as disinterested liberators and then as political apostles buying votes in tribal currency. It had been the place of rejoicing at elections, the place of mourning in defeat and now resumed wounded significance in the Biafran state.

I liked the ones at the Post Office. Its attraction was the certain misery of messengers. Village heralds -the crying voice at night, the warrant-chiefs messenger, man with the gong -had always dressed in tatters as though to remind all that they were mere emissaries and undeserving of death.

The Nigerian post had an office sure to hold dilapidated walls and out-worn leather chairs. It always served coffee, black filthy coffee, by its newspaper corner and hot drinks grew up around those roundtable spots with illegal licenses issued by desperate postmasters.

The post office was locked and boarded up. A policeman told me to turn right back and keep on walking.

"I'm a reporter"

His eyes shone with pride and suspicion. "Which news-paper?"

"BBC"

"Make I see ID Card"

I showed him my old one from the Ministry of Information. He puffed his chest. "So wetin you dey do here?"

"Wetin happen for here?"

It was a long story. We walked while he said it and he had forgotten his beat when I asked of the Railway. Nobody would attack the Railway. It was open. "Even this P.O place but we just wan dey careful. Na why the commissioner of Police, Eastern Region, Nigeria, send me come here."

He told me the routes to the Railway and the State House. He looked thoughtful as I left "How you wan take send your paper now to overseas"

"I'll just fax it"

"Wetin be fax?" I had never seen one but they were the rage in the Ministry of Information. The Dacom Rapidfax had even been in the 1965 budget and entered our offices, through graft, as calculators.

I explained it to this fascinated and lonely man; he clapped his hands in amazement, his voice a fond echo as I walked to the railway "I talk am! White man na witch. E remain to send person inside machine"

In gratitude, he gave me his map and compass. Could I find the true north? My nod was slow.

"Make I show you. As you don teach me something, make I teach you this one" He taught me. It took me an hour with frequent stoop on the roadside but I have remembered compass navigation ever since.

I got to the railway and found a heavy crowd but the policeman was not wrong. The people had gathered to watch the exodus of federal troops of northern origin.

No. One says "people"when it is congress. This was a mob. Tense. Electrical.

It was a sight. There were maimed children, bereft mothers, broken fathers on both sides of the tracks. And over there, their own tribesmen sullen in police or army uniforms -some of them injured by the mayhem elsewhere in the country- protecting these smirking faces burned in sahara. Nobody said a word.

There was enough pain and anguish on the faces of the detail and it was to their eternal honour that they did not harm the northern soldiers.

It would have been easy to walk off the train and let the mob lynch the hausas. It would have been easy to turn their guns upon representatives of those who had displaced and killed and maimed Igbos. But stoic they stood. It was a sight.

I bought some ogogoro, wrapped it in black nylon and went back home. The conversation of gaze is always more poignant. The train left as I did. The crowd after.

I imagine there were fathers staring at the tracks and calling themselves cowards. One always feels like a coward or bandit, never just right, when doing the right thing.

A courier had come from the State Office, Felix told me. He gave me an envolope. In the soliloquy afterwards, he mentioned his pay and how his superior took a cut. I nodded to show I understood and could give no commitments.

CAPTAIN

There are men born into lockstep with the times, a faultless prescience guiding every action, and the captain had been such a man.

His father, the first Nigerian billionaire, had just died and although he was second son, the old man had left immense resources in swiss bank accounts, at the very moment he needed funds for a coalition of Igbo notables and the formation of a new state.

He had grown up among the moneyed elite of new Nigeria, had gone to Oxford to study History, had been Assistant Divisional Officer and lived among the people -things which tend to make revolutionaries of the privileged, like Talleyrand and Lenin.

He had joined the Military and taught tactics. He had lived in the North, understood what he called *the feudal mindset* and in London which was fiercely mercantile. He had been crafted so well by his times and now would craft Time itself.

But this new office, this new posture as statesman and sovereign, felt disconcerting like staring at a face perfectly built for beauty and yet lacking it.

His gravity seemed an exxageration. He had a new reserved smile and his charisma -ever active -was that of a prolific hollywood actor in shakespearean garb and on broadway for the first time.

His accent had nothing of the friendly mix of pidgin which I had known, it was upper class British and seemed even more forced.

His voice had slowed into a trickle, to impress upon the listener, I presume, his command of time. He did not stand when his secretary showed me in.

"Your Excellency, Sir"

"Peters!"

"Colonel"

"But I would always be Captain to you, my friend. There is no higher rank in our affections. Sit, while I round up here"

So Green had spoken to him. I waited. There were phone calls, papers to sign, secretaries in and out the magnificent office.

An hour laster, the Captain leaned back, pushed his glasses down his nose and opened his hands forlornly as if to say "See the life I live?"

"How is work?" I asked him. I remembered he was Igbo "Kedu?"

He grinned, pushed his glasses up again and perused a paper. *"I na-eme igbo gi?"*

"Ana m anwa ike m"

"Onweghi isi obula egburu maka asusu amaghim"

"Terrible"

"My accent or this country?"

These things ooze out a body. *He missed me.* Waved to his desk. "We are doing the best we can"

"How did you find me?"

"Enwerem nwoke nébe nile". He looked up from his papers at my wry glance and he laughed like the Captain of old. "Green called. She was worried you might be living with another woman"

"But Felix's house?"

"Word got around that a British correspondent was in town. You were trailed"

"Jesus"

"Why bring Jesus into this?"

"You barely have enough men to handle the refugee camp. *Ihe mere soro onye nkpuchi obodo?*"

"Because if they don't hear the correct story, the refugees won't stop coming" He pulled his glasses down the bridge. "What do you think we do here?"

"Here?"

"This office. This government. What do you think we are doing here, Peters?"

"Trying to provide order"

Ojukwu shook his massive head. "Order comes from peace. Is this peace?" He thought for a moment, the right words. Herodotus. "In peace sons bury their fathers. In war, fathers bury their sons. You were at the train station."

Well, if that was how he wanted to play this. I quoted Tolstoy "If every one fought for their own convictions, there would be no war"

"To be prepared for War is one of the most effective means of preserving peace. Washington"

"An unjust peace is better than a just war." I had missed a

game of wits. I was only warming up but the elation was short-lived.

He stared at me a long time. It was mirthless, just shy of pain. "You should not say a thing like that outside this office. The people don't know Cicero. If they did, they would give worse than Mark Antony"

He seemed to expect a reply and I offered a "Yessir" in the moment of a door-knock. His bat-man walked in. "Your Excellency Sir" A nod to me "Mr Peters".

"Yes? What is it" The bat-man must have given an imperceptible nod to indiciate that whatever he wished to discuss was private.

Ojukwu rose with a sigh, shuffled past his desk and went out into the hall such that I found myself alone.

The office was a fine affair. Spartan but delicately elegant, the sort of thing one could expect of Lenin or Mao. Books lined the wall and sat on the ornate desk but there was no rich rug, no sofas.

There were ramrod wooden chairs, a small wine cabinet, an atlas against a wall, a terrible portrait of Napoleon, a large rose engraved in the wall with the word *Lily* beneath. A terrible state of affairs.

The door re-opened "Peters I want you dead".

Having said that, he removed his glasses and ran a hand over his eyes. He sat gently, wearily at his head. Then he shook his head and sighed.

I felt sympathy for this man, this man who had taken the burden of Atlas and now sat here, stoic and wanting me dead. It is a silly emotion now but I would have died if it helped the poor man.

I quietly asked "How?"

"Peters, you have been in the Nigerian Civil Service for many years. In fact, I gather, you began there long before I joined the Military..."

"Quite right"

"Information, I believe"

"A delightful place"

We were silent.

"Your files says you speak several languages and frequently engaged in...certain assignations...outside official duties"

"Assignations?"

"Yes. More precisely, I gather you were a scout for sedition. A sort of spy"

I considered his assertion briefly. Would the Governor, no President, choose to interrogate me personally out of nostalgia? "Yes, I suppose so"

"Naturally, we have very few men of your talents, Peters. I want you recorded dead so you cross the lines and bring us information"

I swallowed. I had just come from there and there was a chance the record would become accurate. "I wouldn't be lynched?"

"You? South African? no, no peters, nobody would touch you. Of course, if you don't want it..." he looked crestfallen "if you don't want it, I can't force it on you but Biafra needs you"and he looked at me with such hope that I was at pains to reassure him

"Of course I want it" I didn't "When do I start?"

"Right away. What do you know about codes?"

I knew a bit. I knew what we needed. I was given an office, a measly budget, a small janitorial cubicle in the back of the building from which I wrote memos and trained three operatives. It was a shoddy affair but a heady one, I tell you. I had a purpose.

I told Felix I was working in the Relief Office. I had mentioned his predicament to the governor, I assured him, and it was being looked into but "you know these things take time"

He nodded with gratitude. I remained in his house, using his typewritter for humanitarian requests and it was there I wrote the memo for the "Boys Company" a network of under-age spies useful for the federal incursions we expected.

Nowhere did I ask that they be sent to the front hungry and ill-fed, clutching blood-stained dane guns and Vz.24s against Lee-Enfields, M16s, and Kalashnikovs. Nowhere. But the logic of war goes against the soul.

DOWNING STREET

I had met Sir Francis Cumming-Bruce, British High Commissioner in Lagos, at one of those tedious events by which senior civil servants re-assure themselves of indispensability in governance.

I cannot remember what we were celebrating -there was alot to celebrate in those heady days after independence -but it was in the Sheraton Hotel and our host was the venerable permanent secretary of Foreign Affairs; my ticket was Pius.

There were other diplomats present but Francis was doyen and one got the impression that he considered himself a self-effacing Governor-General of the old british colony.

I was not the only one. I would later hear he repeated the act at almost every event. He would be early although he knew quite well that a Nigerian event always began an hour late, and would man the door or tour the room, shaking hands and patting backs.

Then, having systematically made an impression in every corner -with a weighty remark here and a witty one there -he would excuse himself "for just a moment".

Afterwards he would make a point of arriving just before dinner began with a grave look on his face and a private secretary in tow, would whisper something to this salaried actor who would scurry off with the utmost importance, shake his head with the meditations of Atlas, and promptly resume his bonhomie.

A very important man, the other guests would say. Guardian of this fledgling nation.

When the coup-plotters had settled upon Gowon and Gowon had settled upon secession, it was Cumming-Bruce who arrived the Doddan Barracks in rolls-royce and overcoat to inform the new "Leader" -his government was still uncertain of recognition -that the policy of the White-Hall was the unity of Nigeria.

One could almost imagine him languidly rolling a Benson as he explained in friendly terms that the corporation, for that was what the country was, could not be broken up without risking English displeasure.

Ironsi had drawn some legitimacy from the rump of the cabinet begging him to take over the government but Gowon, well, it was an easy matter to declare the counter-coup plotters as army mutineers, to render his speech of secession illegal and his authority temporary. Gowon behaved.

With the sudden departure of the Northern delegates and the conspicuous absence of the Ikoyi Rolls-Royce, Ojukwu sent me to Kaduna. My brief was to dicover what new proposals would be forthcoming and enable the east prepare but his un-spoken desire was a firm answer to the question of War.

I travelled the same afternoon, careful to arm myself with Roland and Azeem. At the checkpoints I was a south-african on tour. At the hotel, I was an interpreter for the frenchman and Azeem was our guide.

The northern delegates had fallen back to argue their positions against the Emirs. It was connected, this ominous appear-ance of Colonel Hassan at the conference and the sudden dis-agreements in their position.

Francis had come up to Kaduna, Gowon was only front-man after-all, and had spoken with the Sultan and Emirs on the necessity of an immediate volte-face.

The North must not only remain in Nigeria but must render it unitary, defending it if necessary with reasonable force and the certain good-will of the British government.

He pointed out, not unreasonably, that to retructure along the lines of confederacy would destroy the most important resources of the North: central government, southern oil, seaports.

To reassure them, Francis painted the Nigerian Army in warm colours. If push came to shove, the British would funnel such resources as would ensure its personnel were safe and its profits secure.

The Emir checked his sincerity by asking for his personal word that no European power would support eastern secession or leadership and Francis, Benson-Light Francis, blew smoke "You leave that to us. They'll stay".

It was a wise gamble for without it, the North was quite willing to break-away from the nyamiri and the British could not long hope to access Nigerian oil from the entrepreneurial south.

Hassan was a fierce workman when once he had agreed to the principle of the thing. He had pledged that he would set out for Lagos immediately and had arrived at the conference to state the new northern position to a delegation of the popular will. The delegates demurred. They were not willing to act feudal-master over rebellious Igbos.

They sought out Gowon who informed them he must play the role of unbiased peacemaker. Meanwhile, with money and sense and veiled threats, the colonel swung some over to one Nigeria.

The remaining had packed their bags in resignation but they were informed of the lack of this option and given a vacation instead to be guests of the Emir.

The power of a traditional ruler was no longer as great as before the British. Land was scarce, the gifting of women now frowned upon and the Nigerian pound clenched tightly in these courts.

These functions had been taken by the men of the republic, by men like Okotie-Eboh and the parliamentarians -but local chieftains were, still are, the local manufacturers of consensus. Their royal staff of office was public opinion and their unique privilege was ostracism, like the bull of excommunication in fifteenth century europe.

The delegates were promptly beaten into line and I did not know if Francis and tobacco was in the room but I knew they would return to Lagos again as a monolithic bloc resistant to common-sense.

I had discovered the position of the North through a servant-girl in the Emir's palace. Her hijab was neatly folded upon the setee and she was asleep in the passable luxury of the hotel. But she could not answer and I, no prophet, could not see if a war loomed on the horizon.

The Republic trembled on the brink of *what*? Disunion perhaps. Restructuring certainly. But Civil war? What did Francis mean by reasonable force?

Violent language littered the newspapers and blood had been shed but how far would language lead those who spoke with such virulent passion on the streets and at the court and in the conference?

I was hungry. The servant-girl, Amina I think, was an enthusiast. She had repaid my attentions with the fevered gropings of peasantry wishful for a ticket into high-society. I was far from that society.

I went down to the lobby and when I sat down at the bar, against the wall with the mirror in back and dirty mahogany in front and the waiter asked, I ordered whiskey.

Something to burn while the kitchen worked and I asked for the telephone, to tell Ojukwu quiet simply "There would be no freedom"

The Military governor refused to believe me. He had just come off dinner with Gowon and was reasonably assured that the constitutional conference would speedily restructure the country, return the polity to democratic rule and return him to his soldiering.

"Men like me should not be bothered by such civilian trifles as reach my desk each morning, Peters"

"I think Men like you would be needed far longer than you suppose. The British Government has sanctioned the use of force"

"The British government does not have as much say as that ferret-faced High Commissioner would have you believe" he replied. "Moreover, as cooler heads in the North recognise, no region is proposing dissolution. It is a salve to our wounds, a temporary measure, and we might yet find that another constitutional conference a decade from now would propose a firm union. Nobody in their right minds would resist this"

"But what if they do? This is not an issue of debate. They have been given clear instructions"

"Then we must thank God the Emir has no say in the East, West or Middle-Belt"

I pointed out that the Emir did indeed have a say. The army had been cleansed of the Igbos and middle-belters, held no tangible western presence and was stationed everywhere but the

East. "We might find ourselves alone"

"You must think very poorly of me as a diplomat" the Colonel said.

"I think very highly of you as good man"

"Which is the same thing" he laughed. "Speaking of goodness, Green came to me demanding a hundred pounds for your baby"

"It is not my child"

"I agree it looks lebanese but she looked so pitiful that I could not help it.."

"You did not..."

"Think of it as a tribute to happier times" he said.

I did not have time for Green. I asked him what Gowon had said of the weapons which were to return East and he said the fox had demurred.

The one concession the captain threw me was Port-Harcourt. "If you are so worried, there is a man who can help us. "Someone sent me his file. While we buy what we need for our men, he can build something. If he does not blow up first."

I was to type a letter of introduction on the Eastern Region's letterhead, talk with the pilot Egbule and give as much detailed specifications as we could muster to Viragbo.

I could take a small guard from the volunteer force. I would find a file on this indigenous Wernher Von Braun and as many free passes on the Enugu-PH rail.

I thanked him and rang off. I had been a pacifist, I still counted myself one but there was no rational retort to "speak softly and carry a big stick".

I was on whiskey, planning the new assignment when Roland came to me for a blitz of chess. Azeem did not know the game and had escaped the frenchman with a short drive for jerrycans and petrol for our road-trip.

Roland was dark, intense and walked about with a constant sense of foreboding. He had been a lecturer in scotland, an editor in new york, and now spent his days as a faithless journalist in Africa looking to be a french David Wallace.

He was kind, always broke, always up for an adventure and when I told him we could go North to mark the turmoil on my publisher's checkbook, he had thrown some underwear, a change of khaki and a chess-board into his threadbare sack. I felt no guilt.

"Wine?" and I said yes. With his opening move, in what he hoped was a voice with great meaning, he said "Ojukwu is a great governor"

"Yes" I moved my piece "A great soldier"

"A noble man"

We played in silence for some time and I let him gain the queen. "What are we really doing here, Peters?" Ojukwu had asked me the same thing the last time and there was no clear answer.

"What do you mean?" I struck in the fine flourish of a Kasparov. "Do you not see this empty hotel. I came here once and had no room, I tell you." Two pawns were gone. "The Igbos, merchant-men were everywhere and the garden was gay"

"You brought me here to see a hotel?"

"No. To see the loss. Tomorrow we go to Port-Harcourt to see the refugees. It will make a fine story, I tell you. The newspapers in Europe might syndicate it, eh?" I took his queen. "Will you come?"

The food arrived. He gave an embarassed smile and promised he would be ready by dawn so for his grace, I tasked the kitchen again. "Vodka for my good friend"

"There is no vodka" I looked at Roland meaningfully. In response he took my Bishop.

"Will there be war?" he asked me as the waiter turned away.

"Journalists like to pretend they are prophets."I was four moves away from checkmate and it was dawning upon him, slyly tugging his mind into resignation. "Historians too."

"Foreign Office staff too"

"A fine opinion you have of me Sir."Checkmate.

"Well?"

"Another. I cannot sleep"

"Me neither".

We spent the night at the game and when I crept up to shower, Amina was still asleep.

Her serenity was childlike and it felt wrong to rouse her from this momentary comfort so I dropped a ten-pound note next to her burqa and quietly left Kaduna. I would not see it again.

THIS SIDE OF PARADISE

You do not meet many men like Viragbo Menegbo.

Viragbo was absolutely different from the mob of lecturers who had replaced the British academia and replaced it so thoroughly that the University's only merit was the language.

He was a true devotee of the gospel of science, of the eminence of the Royal Society and Patrick Blackett, of the benefits of colonialism.

He was miles above the subscribers to his magazine, miles above the paper-churning mass of other professors, and had obtained a special injunction against his senate presence by pleading insanity.

A real master and a real mess. People came from foreign countries to consult him and invariably remarked on his first-class intellect and mindless filth.

The remarkable thing was his existential disgust for anything human. He reserved his venom for students and subscribers, those persistent hanger-ons, weights around the neck of science, who brought him one invention or the other, hare-brained swarm talking of the eternal machine or a new musical instrument, crowding the passageway with a "Porofessor, this will blow your mind"

And his mind was blown, it was, by the difficulty of crafting new insults for each entrant. He hated them in convulsions, hated anything human.

At the slightest sign of disagreement, he gave free rein to temper and the hapless consultant would be turned inside out, instantly crushed.

There were stories of men who left Viragbo's office and had their wives leave them for incurable impotence. The poor insolent bastard would be let out the door in a daze, only vaguely remembering what his name was, only finding self when he too spat venom against others.

Viragbo was a mad man with disciples.

He was bent with age. He himself liked to remind you of that fact "A man my age", "I have not come this far", "when were you born, young one". He had never been big but now he was small, wiry, a hoary head and small frame with the force of a tornado.

He stayed alive, he said, with british cuisine and walking exercises around the campus with his head struck forward, downward, and God bless the soul approaching his trudge with a "Porofessor".

He had good reason to stay alive: In addition to being artist, inventor, journalist, lecturer, and a gourmet, he wanted to win a Nobel.

He had led a perilous life, one with unnecessary dangers like the nickel hydrazine perchlorate blowing in his face and taking a finger. He felt Newton would not demand less.

I learnt all this on the journey.

This was the man who would lead the Biafran effort for indigenous weapons although his misanthropy meant he was not on the team later named Research And Production organization of Biafra.

These were heady days. There was a secret research unit but

the dissections of human and animal were more concerned with scientific juju than with tribal superiority or descent from Isreal.

We knew Juju worked for dane guns, the spirits knew those well, but they had proven quite useless against machine guns.

Arochukwu shrine, the deadliest shrine in pre-colonial times, a sort of Delphi above the city-state gods and personal idols of igbo hamlets, had failed to stop the British.

One must suppose the spirits were rather awed by white skin, were first converted by the Holy Ghost or could not stand the arms of the Royal Niger Company.

This time senior government officials were concerned with spiritual encryption for units, native teleportation for spies, psychic armour nd telepathy for soldiers, invisibility cloak for airfields and markets, and sennacherib plagues against Federal forces.

We were told it saved the Uli airfield until the very end. We were told the CIA were doing the very same thing. But Viragbo was concerned with an extremely practical matter: the rapid creation of drones.

The Biafran government had siezed Nigerian Air planes at the Enugu Airport as its share of the British heritage.

It had bought used aircraft -some b-25 Mitchells and two B-26 Invaders. It was building a dozen MFI-9s but mercenaries were the most effective members of the Biafran Air Force and equipment so scarce that training required approval from the Captain himself.

Biafra needed drones and it got them, I tell you. They were employed at the battle of Port-Harcourt, pushed back Federal forces three times, and could not defend calabar because battery technology had not reached the genius of Viragbo.

They say Federick Forsyth, great writer and poor MI6 spy,

befirended the Captain for this very reason and the British stole the research, passed it on to the CIA and built the Predator.

I met Viragbo at the campus cafe called Five Fingers. It was an establishment for "swallow", purely native foods eaten without cutlery but the professor had obtained a senate injunction forcing this enterprise to sell coffee and sandwiches.

If he was not in his office, he could be seen in a corner beating his typewriter and sipping scalding coffee and heaven help your greeting.

I dropped the letter of introduction and stood quietly as he stared first at me, then the contents, and again at me. I held the hint of a tolerant smile

"Well at-least you're not stupid"

"No" I answered simply and sat opposite without permission. I was trying to establish mutual respect, not subservience.

He stared more. I blinked amiably.

"What can I get?"

"A few men. A thousand pounds. Any material you need"

"A thousand pounds? What is my assignment, a bicycle? When were you born, young one? I served in Burma and we all heard of the Germans building a massive rocket. We dreamt of its terrors. You think Hitler gave a thousand pounds, you ever hear of the Manhattan Project? I guess not. You illiterates put yourself in a political fix and come throwing a thousand pounds at me..."

"You academics think you are the saviour of mankind but you are as worthless as your articles with its dust."

There are words unholy to tell. After a stunned silence, the professor's curses rang out for thirty minutes in English, Khana and Latin. Students left in a hurry, the restuarant staff sighed, the manager came out and retreated.

Interspered with the insults was a history of the world and the importance of knowledge to statecraft.I sat quietly until he had spent himself.

"Will ten thousand pounds be okay or will you lose your position at this university. Professor, I come as a friend. War is coming. You don't have many friends. There will be lists and it will be a local affair. Do you understand what I am saying?"

"What is my business with your wars and politics? I have never bothered anybody. Go. Get out of here. I like to be left alone. Another can build your drone. Get out"

"Okay. You need someone in Enugu to ensure you are left alone. It would a pity that men envious of your genius deprive you a chance to use it right when a Nobel Prize is in sight"

He was quiet, attentive. "Think about it for a second, Professor. A new state would be recognized by the British Commonwealth. Your success might get you into the Royal Society. The Colonel would be sure to drop eminent names, Achebe and yours for instance, in the right ears. Stockholm has the same politics you so richly despise"

"Stick and carrot eh?"

I shrugged. "You are under no obligation to commit treason against the Federal Republic of Nigeria."

"30,000 pounds. I get to pick the men?"

"Yes. You get to travel free too." I nodded to the men at the next table. "Those officers will support you."

"Support or surveil?"

I did not respond. "How many assistants do you need?"

"60"

"No more than 15"

He looked as though he would explode. "You ignoramus. Get out of here" He was shouting at me and the men by the door. "You think this is politics? You think bauxite answers to votes?" He said it in far worse ways, I tell you.

"15 assistants, Professor. And if you need extra labour, tell me"

When I was imprisoned by federal forces, I learnt Viragbo had sent word to Lagos shortly after my visit.

He wanted a hundred thousand pounds, sixty assistants and assurances of national and commonwealth distinction. He got shot after insulting Federal Soldiers shooting sporadically in the aftermath of the fall of Port Harcourt. We got six drones.

That afternoon I paid a visit, Roland in tow, to my mother's grave at the Port Harcourt Cemetary. A white soul in a sea of black.

She was surprised to see me with flowers, I think, but death leaves the best memories. It is a kindness -this preservation of the sublime, a cleansing of the mortal errors of relatives.

I thought Green might want to come here and croon. Death would be beautiful as everything was to her. I supposed it was a fine habit to see the exotic in the mundane, the magic in a listless afternoon, the south african heritage in a scrapping civil servant -"*my oyinbo government man*"

I did not stay long. I dropped the flowers and poured the libation, then Roland and I headed to a pub to drink the living.

Ojukwu had returned from Aburi, an African Munich, and the newspapers had him and Ojukwu eating out the same plate. Peace, in large fonts. We drank to peace in large pints.

There was fevered hope in the lobby that things would return to normal soon. An Exxonmobil man from the headquarters had called Gowon "a Lincoln with more sense".

This would be an African landmark in statesmanship. Grotius Hobbes and Locke were quoted by the newspapers. The newspapers were quoted by boys. The girls liked the sound of a social contract.

There would be peace and communal love again. By continual commerce, amity would establish what the selfish colonialists had not.

We returned to our room to find a letter waiting for him from the embassy. The British were warning their citizens. It was a diplomatic weather-report, best interpreted as: *Nothing major, merely our civic duty to inform you to return home as there would be no commando rescue, no SAS for your recalcitrance. Atleast get to Lagos.*

There would be no peace.

A SORT OF DUNKIRK

9 August. Three thousand biafrans struck across the Niger Bridge and entered the Mid-West. They wore amulets and faulty weapons and sat atop rickety wagons but they wore the grim look of righteous revenge and the fanaticism of a citizen army. The war had begun.

It happened while Gowon was preaching his swift and concise "police action" against the secessionist state.

Nigerian soldiers had besieged Ogoja in northeast Biafra as a diversionary attack, had taken Nsukka and the Island of Bonny, had announced that the War which was not a war would be over by year-end.

He had disowned Aburi as we had suspected he would but Ojukwu was ready. The state departments had been created months before the declaration of Secession and the formation of the Government of Biafra.

Weapons had been bought, built, given to the recruits domiciled in secondary schools and other make-shift barracks. The S-Brigade had been formed.

The Brigade had struck across the bridge, flung its sentries apart, and captured Warri, Sapele, Ughelli, Agbor, Uromi, Ubiaja and Benin City -20,000 square miles of Nigeria.

They called it the Biafran Blitzgrieg and its spectacular success was preached in eastern churches as the story of David.

David here was Victor Banjo marching across the bridge of Ojukwu, the personification of an Isreali Patriach. *Shall I pursue? shall I overtake?*

The Federal Government was overtaken with turmoil. They had relied on overt propaganda, beaming the fall of several eastern towns which lay sedately Biafran, and upon their higher numbers of trained officers.

Ojukwu that old lecturer of tactics had reverted to guerilla warfare. Ojukwu had secretly trained 3000 strike troops of the S Brigade under Banjo with direct access to his office, and this was only one novel part.

There was the Biafran Organization of Freedom Fighters, which took the function of Russian Cossacks; lone intelligence agents like myself; local militias; and the Boy Brigade -units outside the Biafran Army, Navy and Airforce.

When Banjo reached Ofusu, it was Gowon's personal boydguard who made a desperate last stand and lost. Ore lay open and, a mere 130 miles beyond it, Lagos.

If Gowon thought the war an easy rebellion, he was brilliantly educated. He had his plane scheduled for departure to Zaria. Lagos was desperately under-manned.

But if Dunkirk lost the war for Hitler's Germany, -granting Britain's defense some reprieve and French resistance its impetus -Ore was the same for Ojukwu's Biafra.

A push into Lagos would have ended the war but there was a week wasted in the MidWest and another three weeks at Ore.

The Federal Army embarked on a crash-course for new recruits, obtained British aid and built up the defences of Lagos.

Simultaneously, now fired up with evidence of Igbo designs to take over the country, Nigerian soldiers broke apart the Nsukka trenches and advanced towards Enugu.

There were ten commanders with 110,000 troops on the federal side, men whose names were known across the lines.

Hassan Katsina, Mohammed Shuwa, Benjamin Adekunle, Shehu Musa YarÁdua, Murtala Mohammed, Olusegun Obasanjo, Muhammadu Buhari, Ibrahim Babangida, Sani Abacha, and Theophilus Danjuma under Gowon's leadership.

The best two would be forcibly retired and the remaining eight would begin the dancing chairs of Head of Government for the next fifty years.

Three of the latter would suffer imprisonment and two would be assasinated in office. They would grow from fresh-faced army officers into the wealthy elite of the new Africa.

The Biafran side had Phillip Effiong, Albert Okonkwo, Joseph Achuzie, Ogbugo Kalu, Timothy Omwuatuegwu, Humphrey Chuckuwka and our christened David under Ojukwu's leadership.

The first four, Hannibal among them, would tender the articles of surrender; Timothy would die an Abner, Humphrey would suffer imprisonment

Victor Banjo would be executed by the Biafran Government; his arrest and execution seemed like persecution from saul but the pastors said nothing; there are no victories for the fallen vizier, only the unmistakable stench of treachery.

And he had been ambitious without wisdom. There are many sorts of betrayal but that stemming from idealism is the worst of them. He had done it with the 1966 coup against Nigeria and would attempt it against Biafra.

His attempt at playing Talleyrand cost him his life. He was recalled to Enugu for consultation where he was calmly arrested, gently laid to rest.

I have always ended the biographies of great men before

their reversals. It is a sad thing to see the Napoleon of Umuahia transformed into the yellow-skinned emperor at Saint Helena and Abidjan.

Ojukwu began his purges, restlessly culling or transferring officers, clamping down on minorities calling for statehood and autonomy, raging against a world blind to the justice of his cause.

In between these names and these days of fright, the offensives and counters, are the souls of a hundred thousand soldiers, some two million civilians in mass graves and the momentary or permanent displacement of four million people.

Eighteen million people devastated, left with a worthless currency and a willing Government unable to help beyond 20 pounds each.

A rose by any other name. *Maafa. Kuteketezwa. Mgbukpo.*

THE ASSAULT ON PORT-HARCOURT

The schools were barracks now, holding its former students in different khaki.

Ojukwu had visited the elite Stella Maris, my alma mater. I joined the delegation at the time. He had not come to persuade them, he said.

Merely to explain how the Igbos had been oppressed and he told them they were all igbos. He made the boys laugh and he told the stories of pastors and teachers and children like themselves massacred in the north.

This was a muslim-christian battle, see? He did not want war. Had they not heard of Aburi?

He loved this country but he was entrusted with the destiny of the Eastern region and he could not keep quiet while its people were killed, killed by fellow black men. Even the British had not been so bad.

The teachers had been speaking in their classrooms for weeks. Latin phrases saying "If you want peace, you must prepare for war".

They led the standing ovation, were drowned in its wave. The accent and humility, the prospect of war birthing a new nation, this attendance and influence upon destiny, were too much

189

for the boys. They howled as they clapped.

"Give us guns, we are angry"

The captain always had a way with words. The Irish Principal offered a prayer. A month later, he closed the school and handed the keys to a captain of the 8th Battalion.

The women gave their daughters and food. The men bought drinks for the Biafran army. There was a waiting peace, the sort of serenity one finds before the charge, the last gladiatorial breath before arena.

Calabar fell. A difficult story to tell. It was the first day of things to come. Bony and Calabar fell and deprived us of two ports.

Calabar fell and Port-Harcourt had to be retained at all cost. Biafra would be landlocked otherwise. The Biafran 12th Division under Lt.Colonel Festus Akagha held a defensive perimeter stretching from Arochukwu and the 56th Brigade to Uyo and the 58th.

March 8, 1968, and three federal brigades threw an offensive against Oron and Uyo. The 33rd Brigade occupied the town while Colonel Etuk of the 16th and Lt.Colonel Shande of the 17th pushed through Eket and into Opobo.

Biafran troops were cut off and surrendered to this swift punch. The 15th Federal Brigade stationed at Bonny now launched an amphibious attack against Port-Harcourt.

Colonel Ogbugo Kalu of the Biafran Army had first commanded the 8th Battalion responsible for Port-Harcourt,Bonny, Ahoada, Calabar and Oron.

After Benjamin Adekunle, the Black Scorpion, took Bonny without much resistance, he was relieved of command. Afterwards he was granted the 52nd with the old mandate and the defense of Port Harcourt would prove his finest hour.

Colonel Akinrinade of the Federal 15th launched his attack and secured a beachhead at Onne but an unexpected counter-attack forced them to retreat within 24 hours.

Kalu sent commando units against Bonny in an attempt to recapture the island but reinforcements from Lagos bolstered the 15th and they were repulsed.

In late March and early April, the 15th ceased to exist after Akinrinade surrounded Port-Harcourt and found himself surrounded by Kalu's 52nd.

The Biafran High Command were furious he had halted once the Nigerians had been pushed out of Port Harcourt and the surrounding countryside but he had reason to pause at the creeks with its federal sympathies and difficult terrain.

There were cries of sabotage. Here was another Banjo. Wise officer and miserable politician, he was relieved of command and replaced by Major General Achuzie. He could have died. I protested.

Here was a great officer hounded out of command by civilian envy. What happened to the precept that a General, once given command, had full discretion?

There is a doorway to the British. And Ojukwu was British. A doorway as open as african chiefs at the sight of seaman schnapps -the traditions of egypt, greece, rome and, above these, Sun Tzu.

I had never involved myself in military affairs. I ran my operations as independently as possible, only tapping the military if one of my men had to cross the lines.

To Biafran and the Nigerian officers, I was simply an European gadfly -by turns reporter of the BBC, the Deutsche, the Pravda -and the reason press thrives is because each man wishes his name in print, on radio, captured for television. Go. Come in.

Vanity.

But I took an acception to the Kalu case and wrote for him. I do not think I was the only one but I wrote directly to the State Office, to the captain, to man not state and forgive me if I think I saved him from Banjo's fate.

Forgive me, I tell you, because sometime in your life you will find yourself adjacent to an event of great import. You will draw lines. You, self-important being, unseen potentate, you will draw lines.

Saints are celebrated because others are artists on their behalf but you do not have disciples, apprentices, spokesperson. You will not resist taking the brush. You will say you saved him from ignominy and ensured he saved owerri.

Sure, he lost his command but your letter had an effect. Took some rumination but the diminutive officer would be given the 63rd Brigade staging guerilla assualts across the Nigeria against the Federal 2nd Division stationed at Asaba. After Owerri fell, he was given charge of the 14th Division.

It was a promotion tempered by the presidential letter accompanying it: "Your role in the Port Harcourt disaster is still fresh in the minds of the people. You must clear the enemy from Obinze in 24 hours or submit your resignation from the army".

Definitive sign that friendship affects statecraft. Pericles answers.

And Kalu did not disappoint. He captured Obinze, Eziama and Elelem. Advanced into Owerri and besieged the Nigerian troops while the swedish mercenary pilot Carl Gustaf von Rosen and his "Biafra babies" fighter squadron hounded air-drops.

Only three hundred federal soldiers, survivors of the 16th Brigade under colonel Etuk, escaped the seige. The town was liberated and Kalu promoted to Brigadier.

But Port Harcourt was never re-acquired despite my frequent advice. Its strategic importance was not merely access to the sea but also royalties from Shell Petroleum. It ensured the Biafran government would soon go cash-strapped and landlocked, it could not easily acquire further weapons. If Ore was Dunkirk, Port-Harcourt was Normandy.

The Biafrans knew. The Captain must have found me pedantic. He had tried but academics and journalists were the men outside the ring, insulting the man in dust and blood, the Theodore.

My team was still pulling great intel but it did not matter, Ojukwu stopped replying my letters, memos, and phone calls.

It did not matter because this was no Bletchley park. You could know where the Nigerians were. Their strenght and arms and the local mistresses.

You could know and do the nothing you hated because you did not have the men. And if you had the men, you had no guns. And guns and men with no air support. And air support sometimes but the moral was ever absent.

The captain's ambassadors were polite but they had been converted to the gospel of the messiah's hubris. His commanders were hobbled. Caiaphas whispered.

Achuzie was called Hannibal and he found the Alps manned. After five days of heavy bombing and dare-devilry, the major retreated to Igrita.

It took extra bloodletting, flesh in fire or rotting, the fever of the beaten in hidden children, mutinies and desertion.

When our Captain, the colonel, their President surrendered to fate, the Major and others saw the madness and surrended to the Nigerians. Unlike Kalu, they needed no Daniel.

The gods wanted their libation and if it took surrender, do so, do so, why lose the living and the dead?

A HOLOCAUST BY
ANY OTHER NAME

The thing about war, the glory of it and stress disorder as aftermath, is its certainty.

There was no point considering the good or bad of the sewage before you or the indecorum of crouching behind small children. When you heard a bomber, you simply fell flat.

You did what had to be done. I had read of the gas-chambers at Auschwitz and of people clawing their way up the people they had loved in decent times as they sought to escape the gas rising with death.

There was no morality, only sheer necessity and one trusted his intuition so abruptly that his conscious mind would reboot to find himself in the most awkward circumstances.

This necesarily makes refugee camps one of the most pitiless places on earth. If a father gave his ration to his child, this was not honour but the stark realization of its benefits: that the child was far more likely to escape Federal Soldiers employing all they could as cannon fodder in their advance.

The Biafran soldiers would likely not kill a child for sabotage. The Red Cross was airlifting children mostly. It was pure reason to feed the child and keep the family name whenever this goddamn war would end.

And if another adult stole the ration from said child, it was not a question of ethics but rationality, the certainty that it was easier to bully a child than an equally desperate adult, that there was no way to find the wanted in that sea of faces unless by mutual search, that the family name is unimportnat to the outsider. It is true that there were saints in that camp. None of them survived it.

I was a survivor. I stole food from a boy who must have been a cherub in peace but now held a swollen head over a distended body and certainly did not look like a candidate for survival. I thought he ranked even worse than the saints. I thought my chances still fair.

Besides I was crucial to the war effort. Surely the trolley problem is easily resolved if the single individual pitted against the fifty is a suicide bomber.

And every man would think himself more noble but in that camp, degraded into an animal, squeezed dry of sentiment and doubt, the Good Lord would have kept the two loaves and four fishes for himself.

Three days later, we moved again, this time into an old school-yard. There were not enough classrooms so during the prolific rains, day or night, we all rushed into the few and stood tightly, breathing off each other until the downpour was spent.

Cooking was done a kilometre away, in the bush behind, and only in daylight. The men were organized into hunting and guard duty; we were successful only in hunting wood. Guard-duty had only rusty matchetes and our prayers.

I developed this theory that domestication of animals was due to hunts. Where there were rabbits, the horse became useful. The best hunter was the mounted. Here there were rats and the children with their short feet became best.

A hapless rat would take advantage of darkness to track grains towards the refuse bin which was kept in the centre of a classroom or the centre of the quandrangle. The children it thought asleep would wake up and begin a tumult until they killed it. It was dutifully handed over.

It was now inadvisable to steal their rations for we needed them strong and capable hunters if we were to have any meat.

We were in the schoolyard for two weeks before the Federal troops came. In that time, our camp swelled to three thousand individuals. Some of them were biafran soldiers who had abandoned khaki to survive the onslaught.

They were more worried about the retreating Biafran army, of being pressed back into service or shot for desertion. Some of them were federal soldiers keeping an eye on things and we knew them because they ate with distaste.

But the majority came with only the wide-eyed gaze of the bewildered, that unending glare of one in intuitive certainty and permanent distrust of consciousness that is the international symbol of the refugee: Open-eye.

We said "hin eye don tear" to mean one had seen things which could not be seen. Twain said a mind once stretched by a new idea never returns back to form; war was the most expansive idea.

The cruelty of the soldiers was no surprise, they had been piled thick with pills. It was the inhumanity one saw in oneself that tore the eye, brought this question intruding into the mind at the dollop in his plate or during his shit or during the storytelling where joy reminded one of how fleeting it was: *"na me be this"*

Well, three thousand individuals could not move without bombers coming upon us so the elders called a meeting and we were divided into three companies.

One was to remain, another was to move further west to Aluu, there was an Anglican church with ample space we were told, and the third was to march further along the same road, heading to Igrita.

Then the first would advance, each company hopping forward in broad daylight, carrying a red-cross flag and doing the utmost to look refugee-like. If a bomber approached, we were to lie on the ground and sing christian songs. If we met Biafran troops, we were to run.

The leader of my company was chosen with certainty. This was Kandei, a school-teacher, whose beard rivalled Ojukwu's and had been sighted by Federal Troops in another camp.

The second lieutenant believed that Ojukwu had come to the front, was possibly attempting abdication with refugee cover, and gave chase with some thirty soldiers.

Kandei ran. He was nearing fifty but had spent his days streneously giving cane-lashes to the children of an entire school-district. His heart was good. His fear was true. Kandei ran.

We agreed that any man capable of outrunning the federal soldiers and avoiding Biafran troops had strong skills and was divinely favoured. So we elected the now clean-shaven shool-teacher to lead us to safety.

His first act was to forbid any man he remotely considered soldier or spy to join us. He did so imperiously, walking through his troops and saying "You leave". We did not complain. It was necessity unless it touched us.

It was necessity too that he eat the larger share. That he have a bat-man. That a young lady be attached to him as secretary. That pliantives were saboteurs. All these were certain truths in the circumstance, in such times.

It was neccessary too that when the Federal troops came and

the march cancelled, he was quickly denounced by his secretary as a Biafran soldier, a former double of Ojukwu leading us back to Biafran territory, and shot by her new green and white boy-friend.

It was now that I was conscripted. They had advanced rapidly upon our position that it was unwise to flee and we stayed holed up for two days while the shelling went on about us, watching for the uniform which would advance through the gates, poised to flee any colour if we saw ill-intent.

The Nigerians came with smiles, arrested a few men, shot a few in trigger-happy for-love or in-hate instances and "pacified" us.

For the children, pacification was through extra rations and more play-time although most would be taken as pack-animals. A case of pumping the chicken.

The beautiful women got beautiful things and the aged got medicine. The men were whipped into the army and given a four day crash course which left us even more unsure of soldiery.

The father who broke drill because the sound of his daughter being raped in the next classroom was cause for uncertainty was whipped and informed he would soon have powers to rape another man's daughter.

There was no talk of indoctrination. I was given a faulty rifle and told to fight in the vanguard. What they really meant was that I was to fight to stay alive long enough for them to do the actual fighting.

Uniforms were scarce so we were to advance in our own dress, perhaps with boots or a cap or one half of a uniform to ensure we didnt get shot by our own side. This also made it easy for them to spot deserters who were to be shot. Fight or die.

To impress the point upon we new recruits, a firing squad was composed for recent deserters. It was a solemn affair the very saturday we were to depart.

We were drawn like slaves, chained to the man in front and between two columns of black men. Then in the school court-yard, the first six men were declared dead by the federal major, I forget his name, and they were lined up and they were tied up against large cans and they were shot dead.

I support the death penalty, I tell you. It is proper, if the state is to prevent the resentment of the people who gave their right of eye-for-eye to the beneficence of a government, that it kills the man or woman whose crime provokes such outrage that blood alone would suffice for amnesia.

But what had these six done? They looked more igbo than us. They were obstinate, proud, they walked with their backs straight and hobbled with dignity. These were the men who jumped overboard at Dunbar creek, the straight-eyed children of moses. They knew crucifixion.

Necssity now forced my ace. I was sure I would die if sent to the front and I was tired of this dirty existence and Jesus, this was not even my war. You say I could have exhibited my orisha powers but you are mad, I tell you; an angel in a cesspool is un-seen by God.

I went to the Commander and now informed him of who I was: a British spy undercover with the Biafrans. The field had gotten too hot for me.

I knew the exact location and composition of the Biafran units up ahead but I would need to be taken to Lagos immedi-ately to report at the High Commission. For my troubles, I was stripped and placed in a guardroom. Ah, Egbesu.

If I told them, and certainly they asked after their first at-tempt to march onward to Aluu met a small ambush, I would be dragged along in the rear-guard – a better position, true, but un-wanted. I claimed diplomatic immunity and shut my mouth.

The infuriated captain radioed Lagos. If he had not heard "South Africa" or I not looked it, I should have been summarily shot.

As it was, one had to respect the government's most important ally. My story was plausible. He informed them.

Instructions were to send back to Port-Harcourt to be questioned while Lagos checked my information with the High Commission. He came into my cell with his bat-man

"Pack your things, you dey go Port Harcourt"

"I no get bag"

"Okay. 0600 hours, dey ready"

His coming told me he needed something so I tweaked my offer.

He could radio the Port Harcourt Division that I had escaped. In exchange I will tell him of the Biafrans and where to hit them.

My plan needed only his men and I needed to get Lagos urgently, imperative information you see, and High Command was sure to drag its feet getting to the High Commission.

"If you capture Aluu, no be promotion be that?"

"Yes, to Major" The thought seemed to please him. But another advanced upon it "I fit flog your dispatch outtof you"

"And lose your command for treating the Queen's subject and Gowon's ally shamefully"

His batman now spoke up "Eskis Major, eh, Captain Sir, why does he not tell us and let us see if it matches with our information. The men would be glad of any plan that keeps them alive".

When has the possibility of promotion and popularity failed to woo a man's mind? They had practiced this; this patroculus to the obstinacy of Achilles. To play Nestor, Ulysses, or Ajax? I kept quiet.

"Well" he growled.

"I'm ashamed of you, commander. You are intimately concerned with this small affair when the Federal Government needs to win the war. Send me to Lagos. You'll get your promotion when I arrive safely. That is my word"

Honour was British and I think it did it. I was put on a lorry with the wounded and discharged and sent west in a dead soldier's uniform. Necessity makes you see the blood and bullet patches as badges of honour. Coward.

GREEN

"**I** live in Tahoma". Green had found me.

"The lebanese quarters?"I asked with arched eyebrow. The Captain had said the baby looked lebanese.

"Yes. Will you come?"

"Okay, so where do we meet? And I need your assurances no irate father shoots me"

"What nonsense are you talking. You rememeber Ado Garden?".

I remembered Ado Garden. We had gone there once for its craft beer and highlife on a low budget.

And I sat there frustrated with life and with the woman opposite me talking. Green never seemed to stop talking. Silence was abhorring to her.

But she asked you so many questions, rhetorical of course, non-commital enough for you both to feel your active interest as her soundingboard and yet permit mental space for your own insignificant narrative.

She was doing it now "You remember Ado Garden, don't you darling, well we could go there, can't we darling, oh what a dreadful thing this war has been and I cannot wait to see you again, darling, and darling, I'll bring baby, oh isn't this such a beautiful thing, darling"

Darling grunted. Darling went to Ado Garden.

It was the uniform that did me in -I think it was the baby but Green always appealed to higher notions of justice.

I had had the Nigerian Army uniform laundered and planned to regale Green of my escape through rebel -no one called it biafra anymore -and federal lines.

She had heard I was one of the saboteurs, one of those traitors and a fiend at that because *was Ojukwu not our friend* and now he was in exile in Togo, poor man, good man, and I good-for-nothing father, so what if the child was not mine, what if the war was not mine, I was abdicator-in-chief.

I took the knife up my heart.

I remember smiling. I do not understand the men who are terrified of death. You know exactly when you lose embrace with the earth, there is no pain anymore and you remember your last thoughts quiet clearly like the last words of a fine play.

Talented torture takes you here and back, there and back, until it is a drug and then they do not beat you, they let you want a fix and you lie at first but the mouth is unlocked and the truth stumbles out, a drunk on assignment.

I remember thinking these things and of ceaser's last word worth its fame and in my scholarly disdain of plaigiarism, I said it in African terms

"so na you finally do am, Green, na you...."

And I imagined her saying "Oh but isnt it beautiful, Peters, isn't it beautiful". Ah, Matilda.

ABIKU

DB Paago

Firstborn of paradise and lentil patrimony,
Welcome. Your birthcord infinite, the faint
cysts are a delight; You have not shown
Nightfall's terror, the perturbations of lonely
Souls   -call congress of incarnations
To this ode. Rest, Traveller. Welcome.

And no elegant gibberish, seal primeval
Secrets in taciturn psyche. Recieve,
Recieve this remembrance of fetal
modus -the Einstein syndrome cannot
offend this household and the tomb,
Just your size, polished, lies behind
Without ask of stone and gordian knot
Without placating plaque or liturgy
deformed. Rest, Traveller. Welcome.

Intention, to say the tender body is
Or dream befit, is all you need;
If you will stay and dare the hunt
In nightmare and null-point, the cathedra
Is potent bliss, fair rival to Elysian fields
The nuisance of life compensates resident

Divinity with temporal command.

Rest, Traveller. Welcome.

TRIBE

Regno

STREET CARNIVAL

T hunderclap.

Abacha was dead. People turned on the radios, looked into other faces, asked self. *Abacha don die.* There was a shout.

In 1970, after the uncivil war, the Federal Government of Nigeria had begun a massive reconstruction of the former Eastern Region.

It gave loans to small and medium business, built infrastructure and assisted the new state governments to set up several welfare schemes.

It established free schooling for all indigenes and scholarships to Federal Universities around the country. It used its oil dollars to fund the first prototype of a national health insurance service.

The Igbos were welcome. Once again they flocked into the corners of the country. The Armed Forces Ruling Council passed a decree prohibiting the use of "states of origin" by any Ministry, Department or Agency at all three levels of government.

The Army went on a drive to re-integrate and rehabilitate the old soldiers. There was the promise of a democratic constitution rebuilt on parliamentary grounds.

Or, to paraphrase Vonnegurt, so it didnt.

We know Yakubu was Britain's boy and he may have tried to the good thing, the capitalist thing, the eye to the future sort of thing guaranteed to establish the country as once-again the pride of the black man but there were men like Murtala Mohammed, men who begrudged even the small olive now given, and they ousted him.

Murtala may have been communist. He drove without a convoy, and massacred seven thousand civilians in Asaba in a scene similar to Amritsar and stalinist purges.

He was austere, a real crusader, and his foreign policy was unabashedly pro-communism. All of this was unequal to his ethnic chauvinism.

He got murdered and the Central Inteligence Agency got back its country. Democracy would make things more certain, it was said, and a transfer of power to Shagari rebuilt crony capitalism in it's full force.

Buhari came in, to fight the wildfire of corruption, to have his turn in the chair, to play foil to the genuinely disgusted ethics of Idiagbon. He held the keys to the treasury and made it evident.

He was sent home and a new officer came aboard, the genial Babangida, a military populist and staunch capitalist. When his popularity sank, his ego did too. Maradona had no play.

He left weakness and indecision in his place, the sort of cologne certain to attract a man who had none of those qualities and no love of love.

The opposition called it tyranny and the coalition called it benevolent dictatorship. It was neither. Abacha proved himself a willing democrat when he sanctioned five political parties which elected him candidate.

It was sadism, I tell you; a love of irony, a narcissism in need of hate and when he died, opposition and support shook hands.

I came alive the moment Abacha died. I had been born four years before, had said my "Dada" a long while ago, knew my mother by the morning kisses.

But Wednesday June 8, 1998 had me within the tearful shouts of the street as people congratulated each other on out-living the bastard.

It was my most vivid memory of childhood, an archetypal form as clear as the lynching of a black man was to the police officer in Baldwin's Going To See The Man.

These things, these ineluctable moments, form our part in life's drama. Nature is what we've seen, the force of a single event upon a vunerable instant, leading us to the next and destiny.

I knew I wanted to be wept for like this, with the tumult of the neighborhood wrapped in bliss. No state funeral has the magnificent tremor of street grief.

The crowd was one person, and I had no idea it stretched across Nigeria but it did, across 125 million people, and the feeling was the elation of the sports fan --a tremble so slight but flowing front to back in miniseconds of recognition. *This mattered.*

The dream of politics. No man serves a state out oftemporary rush in ninety-minute games. What drives a man to prominence in a state is a desire to rule the bodies of men while alive and drag their hearts in death. *I wanted that, oh I wanted that.*

It was left to school to render me employable. I found the two oldest professions, politics and prostitution, purposefully absent in our institutions of learning and promptly joined them.

I was told I had to go through the school system and become something before I could make a living at the unmentionables.

On my first day of primary school, every one was asked how

they wanted their something. Prospective doctors filled half the class; some engineering, some law and these were womb-dreams. *What do you think he will become? A she? Well, what will she become?*

There were outliers. A pilot, an astronaut, a couple of pastors, a dozen presidential candidates, modest governors -real jobs.

I said "Godfather" and the wisecrack teacher asked who was my Holy Spirit.

He asked just to be sure. I meant a political godfather and he told me that wasn't a career and I assured him it was. He told my parents when they arrived that I had a spiritual problem.

It was the same way I learned the igbos were the cause of the war, a strange fact since all the teachers were igbos but they taught history as sparsely and misconstrued as the Education board told them or lost their jobs.

They told me igbos were vindictive, a greedy soul-less people, Ojukwu a monster who had sought to divide Nigeria, dear Nigeria to which I sang and pledged each morning; the Obasanjo crossing of the Niger was in our class reader. This country was at peace, reclaiming its promise.

When one first sees history, it is in the vestment of science. History was as sure as the years it spoke of -I had no idea the Julian calender was not written somewhere in the Garden of Eden -and the men who preserved it were pure guardians of truth.

I had not yet met Man or discovered the bias in all his work - architectural design to economics and theory of knowledge. He came to me with race and tribe and religion and I had not discovered self.

History -like this one I write -was a meeting point of events and its disinterested interpretation. *Praise Truth.* Truth is God and he was our God, the sunday-school deity and *pray for those in burqa and error, masquerade and culture.*

There was and is and will be this vast spectacle out in the fields and we, poor humans, are only granted two windows of stained glass from which to watch parade and sunflower and death.

We asked questions but all I heard was a tale already as defective as my own through the muffled doorway of another soul. When one says life is stranger than fiction, one does not comprehend the tautology.

HAMLET

Death does not forgive places like persons. The memories in concrete are the flinching highlights, the afternoons with dirty after-taste.

There were fraternities - Pyrates, Buccaneers, Airlords and Klansmen and Mafians, the Vikings -and they were recruiting your pocket and loyalty. Night cadets, Jurists, Outlaws, White Bishops, and Icelanders would offer a hint. *To be or not to be.*

I joined one because of history, because the country's intellectual leviathan had begun such things and hollywood had its Phi Beta Sigma.

Get flogged with a matchete, drink blood mixed with alcohol, and sing the creed. Simple. You were now the chosen, the select few, member of an brilliant brotherhood with quiet members at the rungs you wanted.

It was not simple. It was rigidly hierarchical and forbade you to be static, unconcerned with the internal tussle, incapable of holding stupendous amounts of liquor.

I and three friends chose to be. It would be called the Nubian Society and modelled after Pike's freemasonry. It's Friday night would be a roundtable, no music or alcohol or women. It would require strict vetting. It would concern itself with African Enlightenment. It did not last.

Fraternities, like states, required money and coercion. A

little imbalance and there was corruption or tyranny. We disbanded amicably.

Then grandmother died. It was my first circumstance of death and I was terrified. I needed to know what to do, how to navigate the essence of grief.

Welcome, you poor soul. Welcome.

When you learn to walk, to see your world, you will hear this greeting often. It will never be joyful.

Because homecoming is one more chance to mourn and, more than anything is, grief is the character of your people.

It begins in the womb when you get three names, nothing to do with you. Three for the birth certificate –as tribe, as surname and a third for English salvation.

Grandparents and seventy-two other relatives you may never meet will add other names to commemorate whoever just died, whatever business or hope ended in despair, desire that tomorrow is less dismal.

These names will recede until a deliverance service for your own grief; but that is in adulthood, after you have welcomed others in pending schadenfreude.

For the moment, slapped on the buttocks, you must give a lusty cry for other people's pain.

Welcome, Barinem.

It begins in school where you learn "Word". The 'word' is more important than the A is for Apple nonsense. Yes, learn the English alphabet but how does that help you insult?

When you stand among your peers at recess, the true mark of excellence, the reputation of wit is in your word.

Pray you have elder siblings or that your family lives with fifteen others in a thirty-two room yard; because somethings defy theory.

Learn and do not cry when a poet with better verse than your novice self says "See your shit like Indian man pepper-soup".

Your peers will laugh. Do not cry at the incomprehensible humiliation. Aim high. Say something like "Your Mama pant na like Jangulova" or "see your head like hammer head of horror". Anything meant to hurt.

Condition the crowd each day by buying treats for those who laugh best against your opponents. The important purpose of this exchange of insult, apart from teaching oratory and the art of bribery, is to increase your capacity for the giving and receiving of pain.

When it pushes the limit, you must fight. Fight with tears in your eyes but do not cry.

There is a clear distinction between the gentleman and the afrikaman. The former will not fight for anything except country. That is the English way, to speak of Queen and country and wear a dour face for everything else.

Here, under the heat of the sun and the temper of pepper, you must fight for parent, tribe, self and woman. Fight for your shoes, for a greeting, for the last fight that did not end well for you. What has your country ever done for you?

If you are born with a soft disposition and quiet spirit, if pepper and hot schnapps do nothing for your aggression, or fear of injury holds you hostage –then your justice must be through the Gods. Not to pursue justice is to welcome further injustice.

When a teacher flogs you, discreetly tear a strand of the cane and soak it in peppery water. Do it while you vividly remember the ache of your buttocks in that corporal moment.

If his hands do not hurt the next day, steal his handkerchief to soak in your urine. Piss in annoyance. If, after a week, he has remained employed and healthy, then your soul does not have enough pain.

Go with a coconut and a piece of paper to those who hold the bitterness of generations in a dirty shrine. They will make him slap a Nigerian soldier who will bring him to his own grief.

The aim is to ensure he humbly says "Welcome" the next time you meet; but if you carry a Hollywood spirit inside that black body and call yourself a Gentleman through those times, you only postpone the pain for yourself, poor child.

All of these prepare you for your first funeral around age ten.

White people go to Museums to see Art divorced from life and stuck on a canvas. Pagans. When you attend that first funeral and hear the things said on the dais and in the whispers of a crowd, you will appreciate Art.

There is a smell stuck to your nose, a cup of palm-wine thrust into your hand, and loud local music for this three-day exhibition.

Give the most cursory look at the pancaked flesh inside the casket and admire the woodwork if that is your thing, but move on to the backyard for that is where Art is.

The female relatives of the deceased will be shorn of their hair and it is a pity nobody buys African hair, but that does not concern you.

The first wife, if it is truly an African funeral and none of these monogamous affairs, and the first daughter, will be stuck to stools in prominent locations as if to subtly announce them as culprits of the murder. Nobody just dies in Nigeria.

As a child, remember you have no obligation to console their grief because you do not have enough of yours yet. So drink your palm-wine and watch their display calculated to convince the crowd of their innocent pain.

You see how they put both hands to the head, and then redeploy the two to the breasts while they shake the head and sing a dirge? That is not real grief.

Until the planned accidents happen –the loosening of a wrapper so that the underwear is obvious, the betrayal of a breast, the convulsive roll on the floor in overwhelming sorrow, the piercing shout followed by a careful faint –until such things happen, she did not love her husband or father.

Leave female business to women. Tell me, Son, who is the saddest man at any funeral? Don't doubt yourself unless you have learnt no grief from this letter.

Look carefully for the man who shakes his head and shouts, "Chei, Life is wicked!" to the nods of a small crowd. The nods are important because any solo drunk can make proclamations at a funeral as a not-so-subtle reminder to the hosts to refill his glass. He is of no account.

But when you see the proclamation and the vigorous nods, you have found the saddest man. He will also be the heir, whether adult son or sibling, to the deceased.

Sometimes there will be two or three such men, each with his crowd and his proclamation followed by the philosopher pose. If the estate is large, there will be many more and none will be drunk because the palmwine is poisoned.

Let us assume your first funeral is a safe one with only one saddest man...

I was hearing voices, having memories impossible to own. They were loud, rambling, a rabbit-hole of unease and I sought help from a university cousellor.

"There's nothing wrong with you"

"But there is" I insisted.

"Do you drink?"

"A moderate amount"

She considered me briefly. "Drink more"

"What?"

"Drink more. Watch cartoons or youtube comedy videos. Go for walks. You a very tense person, Barinem, and I would like for you to ease up on the accelerator a little"

"I came here for good advice"

"And this is the best you can get. People don't like you because you seem a tsunami, the exhilaration gives way to doom. Drink and relax, my friend. You can choose to be yourself of course but what an exhausting life that must be"

See? People wore masks, pick a couple was the extent of my mental health session. And the voices would not stop. *Its just like I told you, the pretense of grief at a burial is evolutionary*

I took drugs. I drank more, fell in love with the warmth of eve and left them cold. There was talk of war and I wondered mildly if I would enlist in the north or the south, play berserker or refugee.

The day I travelled for the funeral, a woman walked up to me at the bus-park. She was ancient and sprightly. She sniffed my hands and gave instructions. "Goodbye now. Remember the son of whom you are"

2000

I have never met a black man who respects George Washington or Nelson Mandela. To relinquish power so hard won was saintly; it was also traditional belief that one ought not to wear haloes among men.

There was no surprise when Obasanjo began pushing for a third term agenda. The man had played saint once and was given a prison sentence. He also had the enviable position of being the best of all who came after.

He could claim to be the indispensable bridge between military and civilian, the common man's representative, a Kruschev after the purge-filled years of a dictator. Hail necessity and its evolutionary guide, father of the nation, Charles De Gaulle of African Politics.

Money came from the excess crude account. It was his money, profits off the economic boom he had single-handedly brought the country through liberalization and the Paris Club debt relief. It was an investment, not theft, and what better proof of democracy than the naira in place of whips?

The senators took the money and played deaf. The rejection stung, a 1945 Churchill, and the statesman pursued farming and theology. He tore up his party card. He became a common man.

The 2000s were the age of the common-man. Kings had ruled and then Theocracries had emerged and afterwards there were States.

The States had shifted, across several poles but now sovereign man was here, the true democracy had begun where every man, and this now meant women and children, spoke in the agora.

Myspace, Twitter and Facebook gave voices to the long-dumb -there was no curator, no civil exam, no censor. Man had ten thousand songs in his pocket. It was a miracle beyond the Jesus loaves.

The common man entered the international stage too as terrorist. The monopoly of violence was broken and the age of surveillance began. Gone were the recruitment camps and the daredevil espionage of western intelligence foiling doomsday; doomsday was here, september 11, 2001, and the recruitment continued unabated through the internet into dorm-rooms.

To undercut the new competitor, the states used torture, killed whole villages of common-men, brought remote technology to the fore, sought to insist on its supremacy but this too was vanity.

The Digital tussled with the national.

It had begun with the Y2K problem. What would happen if computer years programmed in two digits with an assumption of "19-" met the 2000s?

There was hysteria about planes falling off the sky, of ATMs shutting and bank-runs, of billings gone awry. And governments, the ones which mattered, paid tithe to this new phenomenon.

Then it ended with a recession, the Great Recession, bringing back state relevance, regulating the algorithms, legislating backdoors.

Nigeria was small fry. It was impressive, for its level, for having seen the democratic light and paid back debts and aided foreign investment but it was a black nation in the darkest parts of the African continent.

The Europeans had granted Africa her statehood and endured its teenage angst. Now through inter-parliamentary relations, they were teaching the adolescent to play nice. When the Nigerian third term bid failed and YarÁdua became president, there was applause for western parenting skills.

There was the Arabian Peninsula with its ageless significance and Asia with its revanchist duo. The Arab Spring would come from the decade's tremors and economic sanctions on Russia and China would be the new extension of Politics by other means.

There were pressing issues like North Korea and Iran, India and pakistan, the Palestinian problem, the endless wars of Iraq and Afghanistan. Real issues. Black Africa could do its homework quietly in the background.

But Yarádua died. He could have lived and enshrined the rotational principle of North-South leacdership in federal politics. He could have crafted a country. The hand of fate struck; with his demise came off the veneers of civility between the old regions.

The north wanted to keep the power, attached as it were to a corpse and the south had the constitution for a war-cry and the north would yield, okay it would yield, but it would make the power worthless and deadly in the north. Boko Haram entered the scene.

One could call it an eye-for-an-eye, the defining issue of Yar-Adua's brief administration had been the militancy in the Niger Delta and it was heard up north that the southerner had oil money gushing through his veins, wiped his sweat with petro-dollars funneled by government amnesty terms and capitalism's earnest apologies.

Militancy had sought innate benefits lost in the greasy politics of national oil, the other was a jihad, warring against the very soul of the nation, seeking neither division nor remuneration but conquest.

The British asked Jonathan to yield. They would need to play off a conservative sect of the North against the jihadist sect. He did not.

He did not and the war came but it was the sort of thing where boys eye each other and draw a line in the sand and nobody crosses and the boys go home leaving a pointless wound in the earth.

The Jihadists came to Abuja and there were militants there and the weary soldiers brought up tanks and took the streets. Then they called everyone to a peace conference.

It was called a restructuring conference and resident journalists were expressly forbidden to call it a requiem for Nigeria.

Each region now had its trade minister and the common currency was the dollar but they shared a flag and an army and routinely met in the same way the G7 met -a discussion on extraditions, questions on quotas, south african interference, french interference, intraference.

Biafra was announced on March 17 2015 and the next day, a group of northern soldiers politely asked Goodluck Jonathan if the Nigerian constitution permitted an alien to serve as President. They escorted him across the Niger.

The Western Region then sent notice to the Arewa Republic's High Command and escorted alien troops outside the new Oduduwa border.

By acclamation, Jonathan became ceremonial President the same day he was issued the red and yellow passport of the Biafran republic.

A symbolic handshake between him and Tinubu, Prime Minister of Oduduwa, was in the newspaper the next month.

Then Goodluck was assasinated and the Biafran government announced martial law. It happened in the government house, evidence of saboteurs nestled in the new republic.

The reporters had the take ready.

This appears to be a declaration of war by the Arewa Republic to the north, perhaps with connivance of the defunct Western Nigeria envious of Biafra's mercantile success. Sources in Government say there would be vigorous response. One official said Biafra did not draw the sword first but it intended to be the last to sheathe it.

It organized a vast militia and imposed compulsory military service every other year for every citizen above 18. It took away an internet infiltrated by the fulani jihadists. It withdrew its High Commissioner and refused visa applications to a state on its terror-watchlist.

It looked inwards as well. Those tribes nostalgic for Nigerian, individuals with Pan-Africanist desires, communist-leaning corporations with a cosy fulani relationship.

It appointed ward inspectors with broad powers of paranoia in a three mile radius and provincial consuls to suspect the inspectors.

It sacked teachers who taught the Igbos were terrorists and teachers who did not teach the Nigerians were terrorists.

It announced the proscription of all protests and temporary suspension of the electoral process; sent censors to the media houses and placed prominent activists under house arrest.

In the defense treaty of Enugu, it gave a base to Russia. It took delivery of warships from turkey, bought decryption technology from Isreal, asked for S4 missiles. Biafra paid for this by raising taxes and chinese debt.

It also renamed things. I recieved two admission letters, one from the Rivers State University of Science and Technology; another from the Igwuata Provincial University of Science and Technology.

EL DORADO

I was on the verge of joining a political party when the Free States of Biafra was announced. It was the path of advancement, like the Ogboni of the west, and they were actively recruiting in the universities.

All things considered, the Free States of Biafra was no cause for alarm. Nnamdi Kanu's Indigenuous People's Party had swept parliamentary seats after Jonathan's death.

They adopted a new constitution, the principle of devolution and a new national name. They voted to limit their own powers and increase those of the executive.

Yes, Nnamdi Kanu was a brilliant demagogue but all he could do was talk. The new government had him hemmed in a conservative cabinet. There was a new President, a celebrated Ohanaeze chieftain, true steersman of the state.

I felt certain the government would embark on some social measures -national health insurance and lower taxes perhaps - with some harmless diplomatic row with Arewa to please Kanu.

There might be overtures to the Ambazonian movement, certain to antagonize cameroon and france. The British would snub the new nation. Isolated on the international scene and cash-stripped in the domestic, the government would be weak.

The questions were what could come after its inevitable implosion. Arewa could start a new war. Rampant insecurity might encourage a proper peace treaty.

The new country could go full communist, looking to Russia and China for protection. Nigerian Economists were predicting inflation for the Biafran pound, the sort of thing certain to propel a referendum and divide the country into seventy-nine confederate states.

Through the wet season of 2019, the government was merely a thing of newspapers and new flags. Plenty happened in those months but they were distant things, peripheral to our being.

Admittedly they were sensational: Parliament was dissolved; then, in flagrant breach of the nascent constitution, President Madu dissolved the assemblies of the free states. All political parties were proscribed.

They called it a cultural leap. The higher branches of the civil service were swept clean of the old guard and IPP members assumed these offices.

The youth wing, the Nnamdi Kanu Youths, broke up any protest with their gangs and shot a couple of Ohaneaze officials every week.

A little later, an auxiliary security agency was formed from the ranks of the National Directorate of Intelligence. It had no name.

But these were countered by the single fact that the civil and military services still relied heavily upon the minorities.

It was business as usual; one could have his people branded saboteurs but the salaries were still paid and bureacracy, in its careful pace, meant the system would outlast this moment of molten lava, would expand with its end.

Ministers of war, trade and foreign affairs -emblems of full sovereignty -had been appointed but these were men no wiser than their days as commissioners, student union leaders, party scribes.

Yes, signboards had come down and back up at the utility companies and government agencies. The electricity and internal revenue board, road safety and police were bearing the name and color of Biafra but they still held their gross incompetency.

A few roads had been renamed but the travellers were the same. The ardent corruption was firm consolation, I tell you.

The Ken Saro-Wiwa polytechnic had been upgraded into a full-fledged university granting bursary and reasonable third-world education but renamed the Philip Effiong University. The man was cancelled from history books.

The successful revolutionaries did not know what to do with the state but they had this certain intent with the 'revolution' *the impossibility of another revolution.*

I discovered that the party could no longer accept applications from the Ogoni. I could not write either. The Biafran Social Review had made it clear what sort of histories were acceptable.

This was not censorship, merely the manufacture of consensus. Anti-biafran professors were untouchable, although the NDI could politely call upon a vehement specimen in the dead of night.

This was not censorship but the next generation must churn out research suiting government's narrative or find their career stalled. It was self-evident that the next generation could not belong to that class of vermin not committed to the growth of the Igbo race.

There was bomb discovered at the Onitsha market and the media advanced. *Sources are pointing to the growing confidence of Ogoni and Kalabari separatist movements, especially on the island. The government has announced a curfew on certain parts of Ogoni-land.*

My ethnicity meant my papers had to go through a censor, never did, and I was granted a friendly hint by an NDI agent that publishing overseas would be considered unwise until I had resolved my issues with reality.

Another bomb. This time in a catholic church at Umuahia. The government issued national ID cards and created an ethnicity watch-list. *Citizens from suspect tribes have been encouraged to limit themselves in certain areas to avoid unwanted harassment. The government in a statement released wednesday said the measure was temporarily necessary to protect critical state infrastructure.*

I had become more careful with my colleagues and students. New faces stumbled in mid-semester and these were the ones avid for friendship.

The men brought gifts and rebel murmurs in a drinking session. The ladies offered their charms and visited my studio apartment.

I did not turn them away. Better to leave the door open than hear a midnight knock and *"a few questions down at the station please"*.

Professor Irome had spoken too freely at a wedding party and had disappeared. Faculty were denounced by colleagues, students and non-teaching staff.

One graduate assistant had visited a lecturer and said something in the presence of a patriotic maid; the two were bundled the next day -*squealing tires, the crunch of boots on grass, the door knock, the "me, what have I done?", the "there must be a mistake" which is a rookie mistake, an Alexandr Solzhen mistake, the door bang, crunch of boots on grass and timid shufflings in-between, squealing tires.*

It was a period of intense suspicion. Neighbours peered into the face of the children, the postman and colleague, yours, and offered a tentative smile.

*You like this government, abi? These times, good times Ha en-
weghi ike mebi anyi. chere ka i bu anyi.* A frown is evidence is
subversion.

Sometimes the NDI only came to give you a hint. That is they
left without the shuffling although all other details remained
and the victim would feel, not relief, but an anguish at missing
the rapture.

The neighbours would shun you; some with outright hostil-
ity at the newly baptised subversive and others, apologetic, shy,
with that tentative smile because one could not certain that he
had not be planted. *We are Biafrans.*

It was a stench and the corner-store girl would speak louder
to you anxious to establish her innocence in a mundane transac-
tion.

A fine puritanism had engulfed the country, I tell you. It de-
manded severity, abstinence from the pleasures of life, attention
to one's duty, patriotism, loyalty, honesty, self-denial

The pastors and priests had new anthem-*was it not division
which brought the British, the Fulani? Unity is the second coming
of Jesus.* And what about the riverine vermin? *Handed over to
perdition.*

Its Calvin was Kanu and for a heaven there was promotion in
the party and state. The Biafran puritan could hold no opinion
outside the party and needed no privacy if his hands were clean.

Illicit pleasures could be anti-Biafran depending on your
choice of consort or dealer. Puritanism made it clear however
that provided you did it with a fellow biafran and did not allow it
interfere with your duties to the state, your sins could be wiped
clean.

There was also a "personal" life without need for ablution,

after a certain level. Senior party members could keep a harem and enough alcohol to drown a village because the responsibilities were great. Work was salvation. It required communion.

Given the proper tribe and enough years of service, you could travel abroad often, even to Arewa. But these privileges were the scandalous items of the newspaper article reporting your arrest for gross corruption after a fall from grace.

Conscientious parents forever educate their children for the era that is just over. There were many of us who would have been functional in Nigeria now stuck out of sync in Biafra.

Our western education did not assist; the igbos were mercantile and a nation fashioned in their image stamped such traits upon "liberty" or "pan-africanism".

Capitalism meant party-stake. Money had right, companies were alive, a citizen had ratings because money pass money.

"Do you know who I am"

"No. What bank?"

The calm superior indifference with which we intellectuals had watched the events of 2019 was now dumbfoundness.

When it was announced that non-members of the Nnamdi Kanu Youth or other party-sanctioned societies would pay full tuition and suspect ethnicities could only school in their region *to protect critical state infrastrature* there was no protest.

I withdrew.

FOUNTAIN 33

The water fountain upon which I sat had been a sixty-two million pounds contract awarded by the Supreme Leader in January.

The Ministry released 58 million. Processing charges, I tell you. University corruption gave the contractor 50 and inflation made that worth 35 million.

Inspector palms were further greased and specifications reduced until the new 33 built a beautifully useless fountain.

The senate resolved to place a safety sign and everybody went home satisfied with the commonwealth and fountain 33.

Here I discovered solace. It is a heart-wrenching thing to look at a magnificent edifice in the moss of uncompleteness and I do not blame the students for avoiding the new fountain like a plague.

Not that people knew of its existence. I had searched "picnic random" on my GPS console and my car had driven me here.

I marveled at that thought. It was not enough, this miracle of navigation via GPS, one could now attain his intention before he discovered it.

They called it the zoo, partly because it hosted lizards and the rejects of society, men like myself. *Suspect ethnicities* were not allowed to attend the day classes or enter the library but we could wear a visitors badge and watch those who did, beg them for crumbs, wait for the dusk.

The picnic lady was sent away by security, informed it was poor taste for pure biafran blood to mix with the riverine. She looked relieved as if the stranger had done her a favour. It was the last time.

I ate bread and peanut butter and wondered when the rations would come. There was talk of a hot war and I wondered if I could survive without attaching myself to some great man, an Ibo stalwart.

That was hard. Every good biafran had to hate the riverine, that insidious blight upon pure igbo blood but I had ideas.

The Zoo suited me fine. The internet was a bit faster and the few unrestricted sites still held knowledge. After the picnic I had visited often, a place for thought. I could apply to be cleaner. No.

The conversations at the zoo were insightful, a pariah network, and it gave me another avenue. I heard stories of rejects redeeming themselves through laban apprenticeships. It was slavery and a glimmer of light. There was free evening school for them.

If I had not done so good by myself, why, I could find a patron and grow up in his trading house. 14 years and the possibility of freedom, a chance at Joseph.

And it was at the zoo I first encountered a bum in danshiki with furtive glances. *No, before. I had dreamt, no I had not, had I? A shadow at the administrative office last time I met it?*

The problem with the mad-man theory was the voice. This was not the voice of a bum. It was deep, flowing, resonant even - the voice of a man with nights of whiskey and cigars.

So here I was enjoying a lunch and private thoughts of joining the resistance or an apprenticeship when the danshiki-bum turned to me and asked

"Are you not tired of the sea?"

Wake.

Made in the USA
Middletown, DE
12 August 2021

45224273R00144